# Christmas Ever After

Elyse Douglas

**COPYRIGHT**

*Christmas Ever After*



This is a work of fiction. Names, characters, places and incidents are either the product of the author's imagination or are used fictitiously. Any resemblance to actual persons, living or dead, events, or locales is entirely coincidental. The copying, reproduction and distribution of this book via any means, without permission of the author, is illegal and punishable by law.

ISBN-13:978-1490545196
ISBN-10:1490545190

There are two ways to live your life.
One is as though nothing is a miracle.
The other is as though everything is a miracle.

~Albert Einstein

To Nickie and Bertie: a little Christmas present.

# Christmas Ever After

# PROLOGUE

It was the day after Thanksgiving. The first snowfall of the season had begun around noon, quickly blanketing Willowbury, a cozy New England town known for its revolutionary war history, covered bridges and picturesque landscape.

The Cards N' Stuff Gift Shop occupied both floors of a gingerbread-style building located on Main Street, between the town drugstore and the library. It was fortunately positioned near the town square, the Willowbury Duplex Movie Theatre and the entrance to the interstate highway.

The shop was successful and thriving, especially now that the busy season had started. Its wooden floors creaked as customers crowded in, picking through sales items and roaming the narrow aisles, eager for a bright, discounted discovery.

Twenty six-year-old Jennifer Taylor, the owner and manager, stood near the window in her back office, alone, her arms crossed tightly against her chest. She stared blankly into the falling snow.

It was nearly a year since the death of her fiancé. Lance had died on Christmas Eve, the night before they were to be married. It seemed like weeks and it seemed like years. Already, Lance was becoming a half-remembered fiction. How could that be? She could easily recall his warm, generous smile; his long sandy hair; his dancing brown eyes. Yes, all of these she could still remember. But the sound of his voice and the scent of him—that unique alluring scent of his hair and neck—were dropping from her consciousness, like stones falling through murky water into sightless depths.

Christmas Eve. Only a year ago, yet so long ago. So far back into the past. So close to her still-aching heart.

They'd planned a beautiful wedding, making all the arrangements together: the church, the reception hall, the food, the flowers, the decorations, the limo. After a big send-off, they were heading to New York City for their honeymoon. The trajectory of Jennifer's life had seemed assured—all things were going according to plan. Then she'd heard the news: the impossible, terrible news. Lance was dead. And just like that, her life, too, was over.

Jennifer stared into the white face of the day as dogs barked, kids ran for sleds, and plastic snow shovels scraped paths across sidewalks and driveways. It was a swirling, rich snow that quickened holiday hearts and herded bargain hunters into malls and shops.

Three inches of snow had already accumulated. Jennifer paced her office, peering miserably into the white wonderland. Through the closed office door, she could hear the murmur of bustling customers; the Christmas music; the constantly dinging shop-door bell, tolling the entrance and exit of shoppers. But she ignored them; she shut them out, as she had now for days. Perpetual restlessness had made her edgy and short-tempered. She felt a tightness in her chest. Her thoughts raced and then knotted, her forehead and neck were always damp. Christmas was coming and she had to find a way to survive it—and all she could see was an infinite blackness.

"The first year is always the worst," a therapist had said.

Jennifer continued to stare strangely into the blur of snow, as if searching for some sign of understanding, some fragrance of wisdom, but all she felt was anger and bitterness. She cursed the snow. She cursed her life.

"Ms. Taylor… "

Startled, Jennifer twisted around toward the closed door. It was her assistant, Angela.

Angela knocked. "Ms. Taylor? I need help. It's really busy out here." Jennifer heard the strain in Angela's voice.

"Yes, yes, I'm coming," Jennifer said, irritably.

In a drooping despondency, Jennifer sank into her office chair and buried her face into her hands. How would she get through another day? How could she get through Christmas without falling apart?

"Oh, God, please help," she heard herself choke out. "Please, help me."

Jennifer's words pierced the boundaries of ceiling and walls and hovered for a time above the roof, near the chimney. As the rising smoke curled skyward, Jennifer's words caught a spiraling draft and they sailed high into the infinite scattering snow, far beyond time and space.

In a land of dazzling sun and glittering emerald sea, the prayer splashed into the water; bobbed and drifted toward the shore. It washed up onto a broad wide beach like a message in a bottle.

Someone retrieved it; someone who had been watching Jennifer for a long time; someone whose job it is to retrieve such things, a kind of sky beachcomber searching for buried hopes, lost wishes and pleas for help. The message was retrieved and delivered.

# CHAPTER 1

Jennifer pushed herself up from the chair, took a hurtful breath and adjusted her slouching posture. She shoved open the office door and returned to the Christmas shopping frenzy.

Cards N' Stuff was crawling with enthusiastic customers grabbing Christmas ornaments, wrapping paper, colored bows and boxes of Christmas cards marked down 10 percent. Jennifer and Angela worked in a hectic flush, as kids careened around corners and adults exchanged lively holiday greetings.

Out on Main Street, the Mayor of Willowbury, J. D. Hartman, held the arm of his wife, Gladys, as they walked purposefully, working their way toward Cards N' Stuff. Snowflakes frosted their hair and covered their shoulders.

Mayor Hartman was a robust man, with a winning smile, heavy face and aggressive manner. He charged through life enthusiastically, grabbing big chunks of it as he went. He'd grown up in Willowbury, gone to Russell College nearby, and married his high school sweetheart, Gladys Walker. Willowbury was his passion and his extended family.

Gladys was petite, with short, grey-and-black hair,

friendly dark eyes and a personality so competent and quietly strong that many believed she was the reason her husband had been elected to a second term.

Gladys and J. D. promenaded down the street, smiling and waving to passing shoppers. They were also arguing.

"I haven't seen the snow plow," Gladys said, with a hint of a challenge.

"The snow plow is out, Gladys," the Mayor said, bracing himself against wind, snow and his wife's words. "I just talked to Dan, and he is out here—in the thick of it—hard at work."

"Obviously, not on Main Street," Gladys said. "You'd think he'd start on Main Street."

The Mayor adjusted the collar of his black cashmere overcoat, squinting in mild annoyance at his wife. "He started out by the highway, as per my instructions. He'll be here presently."

"After a stop at Shanahan's Bar for some holiday cheer... or two or three," Gladys added, wryly, gripping her hat and bending into the wind.

The Mayor bristled. "Now, Gladys, Dan is a good man. I appointed him myself and you have no cause to criticize him like that. You, who can be so generous and charitable. You, who have fought to improve day-care centers. You, who have organized teams of volunteers to tutor the illiterate. You, who have…"

Gladys cut him off. "Cut the speech, J. D. I call it like I see it."

J. D. nodded firmly, as if he'd won the debate. "All right, then, enough said."

Gladys pointed toward the shop, where a steady stream of patrons was entering and exiting. "Look how busy she is. It's the busiest shop around."

"She's a damn good business woman," Mayor Hartman said. "It's a good thing she doesn't have much of a personality. With her business skills and talent, she could run for Mayor and beat me."

"But when you look at her, it's so obvious there's something missing in her life," Gladys said. "She's attractive, if she'd just fix herself up a little. She doesn't look happy, and she's always alone."

"She wants to be alone, Gladys," Mayor Hartman said. "We've invited her to three parties and she's turned us down every time. But this time, I'm not going to take no for an answer! I'm going to invite her personally."

They approached the front door, grinning, shaking hands and making small talk about the weather.

They drew up to the window displays and nosed forward. "Just don't be too forceful with Jennifer, J. D. You know how you can be."

The Mayor passed his wife a sour glance.

The left window depicted a happy family, blushed and perky, dressed in red and green, caroling around their upright piano. Little embroidered red stockings hung by a glowing fireplace, and beside the twinkling Christmas tree, a black and white dog howled, obviously not a music lover.

The right window showed Santa and his reindeer sailing through a deep purple sky of falling snow, over a Victorian Christmas Village, where gleeful, rosy-cheeked children pointed skyward. An electric train circled the village, tooting and puffing smoke, passing ice skaters and carolers.

"Charming," Gladys said. "Very charming. Where did you say Jennifer is from?"

"A small town in Tennessee. Went to college there and majored in business. That's about all I've ever been able to get out of her," J. D. said.

"And she moved here in April?"

"No, March. Came here in March."

Gladys led the way into the shop. As she pushed the door open, the little bell "dinged."

Customers pushed in and squirmed out in a steady stream, packages rustling, boots shuffling, hats and shoulders sprinkled with snow.

Inside, Gladys lifted her nose to the pleasant surprise of mildly spiced potpourris, scented candles and fresh pine coming from the decorated Douglas fir Christmas tree. The Mayor pulled his way through the crowd, nodding and grinning, pumping hands, delighted to move his bulky frame through the bundled bodies and stubborn customers. Bing Crosby sang *Silver Bells* from a CD player.

Gladys caught sight of Jennifer, who was presenting a music box to a weary and conflicted young man. Her thin shoulders sagged, as though some heavy burden weighed on her. She wore no makeup, and was dressed in a frumpy brown sweater, loose dark slacks and scuffed black boots.

Jennifer was attractive and slender, but her good looks were betrayed by a chilly demeanor and guarded insularity. She had chipped green eyes that were dulled and brooding, as if each moment held some freshly remembered melancholy—some old resentment that soured her on the world.

"I'll take it," the man finally said. Gladys watched as Jennifer handed it to the man and turned to help another customer. She was stunned to realize that this attractive and enterprising young lady gave the impression of being a woman old before her time.

With no hesitancy, Mayor Hartman advanced toward Jennifer. A fidgety middle-aged man examined a delicate Christmas ornament that Jennifer held up for his approval. He approved. He took it, pivoted and aimed for the cash register.

"Jennifer Taylor, how are you on this fantastically busy and snowy shopping day?" Mayor Hartman asked, with a broad grin, hand outstretched.

Jennifer turned unsteadily. "Mayor Hartman! What a surprise!"

She took his meaty hand, and he pumped hers so energetically that Jennifer nearly lost her arm. "Can I help you find something, Mayor?" she asked, with a forced, tired smile.

The Mayor indicated toward Gladys, who waved and grinned brightly.

"No, Gladys takes care of all the shopping. Always has. Just has the gift for it, no pun intended," he said, quickly, laughing loudly at his own joke. He turned serious, his broad bushy eyebrows lowering as his eyes narrowed. "Now, I've come to personally invite you to our Christmas party, which is going to be held on December 22nd. Gladys is known for her Christmas parties, far and wide. It's the event of the year and we want you there. And we won't take no for an answer."

Jennifer looked down and away. "Oh, well, I'm going to be busy that night, you see I..."

Mayor Hartman cut her off, shaking his head. "No excuses, Ms. Taylor. You can come by for an hour or so; and I will consider it a personal insult if you do not."

Jennifer struggled for a clever excuse, but faltered. "Well... I'll try. It's just that I'm so busy here, and there is so much to do this time of year."

"No excuses, Ms. Taylor," he stressed, his forefinger

pointed up and wagging. "No excuses. Come and meet the local business community. Eat, dance, drink eggnog and have some fun. It'll do you good.

Jennifer just wanted to get rid of him. "… I guess I can…"

The Mayor interrupted. "Of course you can! Excellent! It's a date then! I know we sent you an invitation, but I just wanted to come in person to make sure you're going to join us."

Jennifer managed a strained smile. He was the Mayor, after all. It wouldn't be good business to alienate him. "Thank you, Mayor. So nice of you to stop by."

He shined with enthusiasm. "We're going to have carolers, prizes, a live band and many other surprises. You'll have the time of your life, Ms. Taylor! I guaran-damn-tee it!"

She looked about awkwardly. "Well, doesn't that sound like fun," she forced out, half-heartedly. She motioned toward a group of people. "I guess I should be getting back to my customers... so many things to do."

"You go right ahead, Jennifer. Don't let me keep you one more minute. We look forward to seeing you soon. Don't forget now, it all starts at 7 p.m. sharp on December 22nd."

Jennifer nodded and slid away toward the window displays, where a pugnacious boy was reaching for the flying Santa Claus.

The last customer of the day was the most difficult. He was portly, spiritless and adversarial. She presented him with gift ideas for his wife, and he shook them off like a pitcher shaking off signs from a catcher.

Jennifer brought out a book of Christmas poetry.

The man's lips thinned in irritation. "A book of love poems? No way. She doesn't read. She watches TV."

Jennifer grabbed a snow globe, filled with a beautifully hand-carved manger scene. She shook it and held it up to the light. "Isn't this beautiful?"

He snorted. "Don't like it."

Jennifer felt her blood pressure shoot up. Three additional gift ideas were all nixed, brusquely.

Finally, he bought a chocolate Santa Claus, bit off the head, chewed it vigorously, and left the shop in a huff.

At 7:16, the last customer finally left and Jennifer gratefully locked the door. A welcomed silence descended, broken only by the hollow toot of the electric train in the window. Jennifer and Angela sat hunched in back of the shop on wooden stools, massaging their aching feet and sipping tea. Nat King Cole was singing *The Christmas Song. "Chestnuts roasting on an open fire. Jack Frost nipping at your nose…"*

"Angela, please turn that thing off," Jennifer said. "I am sick to death of Christmas music already. I don't know how I'm going to make it to Christmas. Do people really like that stuff?"

"Yes," Angela said, reaching up and turning it off. "Most people really love Christmas carols."

Angela Garcia was 22 years old, perky and ambitious. She was full-figured, with long silky black hair and ready dark eyes. Her wardrobe and jewelry were colorful and trendy. She loved makeup, and used an abundance of blush, shadows and creams, spending many happy hours shopping for it, applying it and experimenting with it. If Angela was an artist, her face was her canvas and her makeup was her palette.

"I suppose you love Christmas music," Jennifer said,

wearily.

"Yes… I do."

"Figures…You're the type."

Angela rested her head on her hand. "I think I'm going to get my father one of those gold pens. They've been selling really well. He hates computers and he loves writing letters to my sister's kids in Florida. He gets so bored just sitting around, but his heart isn't very good and he can't do that much." Angela paused, waiting for Jennifer to say something. When she didn't, Angela continued. "My little girl wants a new Barbie doll, of course. Those things cost a fortune, but that's what she wants, so what are you going to do?"

Jennifer's face turned darkly private. She stood up, reaching for her boots. "Let's finish up in here, okay? I'm really tired."

There was long icy silence as Jennifer pulled her boots on.

"I don't really want to know about anybody's shopping," she added. "I'm just so tired of hearing about everybody's kids and everybody's boyfriend and everybody's cute little cat and dog and bird, and everybody's family. I am just sick and tired of it all."

Angela sat quietly for a moment. When she spoke, her voice was a wounded whisper. "Okay…"

Jennifer drooped, as the wind howled around the building. "And now all this snow. We never got this much snow in Tennessee."

Angela took a peek out the nearest window. "What are you going to do for Christmas?" she asked, tentatively.

Jennifer leaned back against the wall, releasing a sigh. "I'm not going to celebrate Christmas. I'll celebrate when it's over, because I'll be able to sleep an extra half hour in the morning and close the shop on time every night."

"I never knew anybody who didn't celebrate Christmas."

"It's a waste of time."

"But it doesn't take time. I mean, you just kind of celebrate as you go about your day. Then you just get with your family and friends and have fun with each other."

"Well, that's nice," Jennifer said sarcastically, dropping back down to the stool.

Angela lowered her voice and looked down. "You sound like that guy on TV," she said, quietly. "The one who hates Christmas. Scrooge."

"Let's just drop it, okay?" Jennifer snapped. "It's such a silly story. Life is not like the movies. Life is real and hard and sad."

Angela stared at her sympathetically. "Then why not celebrate happy times when they come?"

"Because charging right behind the happy times is ugly reality, ready to kick you in the teeth."

"Do you really believe that, Ms. Taylor?"

"Yes, I do. But hey, Christmas is good for my bottom line, so I'll certainly celebrate that." She hoisted her mug. "Cheers."

Angela looked at her, trying to understand. "I always feel happy at Christmas, like things aren't really so bad and that the world is basically a cool place. You know what I'm saying?"

Jennifer stared, coldly. "No. The world is what it is and a cool place it isn't. A cold place it is."

Angela continued, lost in her own thoughts. "Sometimes, at Christmas, I even think I'm going to find the right guy for me and Mariah. At least, it's a dream I have."

Jennifer barked a laugh. "The only dreams you're going to get in this life are shattered ones. That's all the world has to offer. Believe me. I've lived long enough to realize that."

Angela slumped forward, dispirited by Jennifer's words. "Does your family feel that way?"

Jennifer took a long, thoughtful sip of her tea. "I don't have any family. My parents are both dead and I don't have any brothers or sisters."

"That's so sad."

"No… that's just the way it is."

"Don't you ever want to get married? Have a family?"

Jennifer's eyes grew distant and reflective. She blinked a couple of times as if to clear them. "I almost got married once… that was enough."

"What happened?"

"Nevermind. It didn't happen and I'm never going to make that mistake again. I'll leave all that to giggling girls, who have nothing better to do."

"But what about children? Don't you want some?"

"There are plenty of those already. Just look around. Then look into the faces of most of the parents and you'll see nothing but stress, exhaustion and regret. When the kids grow up, they're even more trouble—and they cost a fortune!"

Angela straightened, feeling challenged. "I don't regret having my little girl. It's the best thing that ever happened to me."

Jennifer turned away from her. "Whatever."

"I didn't know you were so, like, cynical."

"I am not, like, cynical. Wait until …"

"What?"

Jennifer hopped off the stool. "Forget it. Let's close up and get out of Christmas fantasy land. It's starting to make me nauseous."

Angela sat quietly for a moment, then worked to brighten the mood. "I saw you talking to the Mayor."

Jennifer went to the cash register. "Yes, he invited me to his Christmas party on the 22nd."

Angela leapt off her stool, excited. "You're kidding me!"

"Nope."

"You are so lucky! Their parties are so cool! I mean, that's what I hear. I've never been to one."

"I'll send you in my place," Jennifer said, jokingly, batching out the cash register. "Can you be here early in the morning? We need to rearrange the shelves and restock those Santa Claus dolls that everyone seems to be buying."

Angela hurried over, incredulous. "You're not going to the party!?"

"Of course not."

"That's unbelievable! It's like the most awesome event of the year around here! Only the real cool people get invited."

"Well, I'm not cool and I'm not going to that silly party."

Angela frowned. "You sound so … like jaded or something."

Jennifer looked up, unable to control her irritation. "That's it. I can't take this conversation anymore." She faced Angela, gesturing for her to stop. "Please, Angela, just get your things and go home! I'll see you tomorrow."

Angela stared down into the glossy wooden floor.

"Do yourself a favor, Angela. Learn to live in the real world."

Angela crossed her arms. "I do live in the real world, Ms. Taylor, but my real world seems a lot happier than yours."

Jennifer glared. "Go home."

After Angela left, Jennifer deposited the cash in the safe, completed her security check and turned off the train, which had continued to make its endless rounds around the track. She gathered her down coat and started for the front door, switching off lights. As she opened the front door to leave, she heard the tiny ring of bells. She paused, turning back toward the shop. As the bells faded, she heard a woman's voice—singing.

"*We wish you a merry Christmas, we wish you a merry Christmas, we wish you a merry Christmas and a happy New Year!*"

It was a soft voice, falling around her like mist. Jennifer released the doorknob. She stepped back into the shop, peering into the darkness. "Who's there?" she whispered. "Who's singing?"

The voice fell away into a loud silence.

"Angela turned off the CD player," Jennifer said to herself, gently puzzled.

She crossed to it, letting her careful gaze settle on it. The power was off. Definitely off. No red ON light. No sound. Apprehensive, she went back to the front door, opened it and passed a final uneasy glance into the shop before leaving.

Outside, the night seemed harsh and endless, the wind frigid and sharp. It howled through the trees like a hunting animal. Jennifer tramped through the snow toward her car, hunching her shoulders, turning her head away from the wind.

She stopped abruptly. Was that the singing again,

coming from inside her shop? She took a ragged breath and coughed. Her pace quickened and she nearly slipped and fell.

At her car, she yanked open the door and slid behind the wheel, shivering. As she drove past her shop, she didn't give it a final glance as she usually did. She just kept on going.

# CHAPTER 2

That night, Jennifer sat alone in her two-bedroom condominium, staring blankly at the flickering television. She reached for the remote and surfed the channels absently, sipping white wine and feeling the familiar dull ache of loneliness. She finally turned off the TV and stared at the empty room, which seemed alive with quiet.

Christmas was coming, and all the old memories of Lance would come crashing in on top of her. They'd already begun. All she could do was make sure she stayed busy, and not allow any idle thoughts to intrude. It would be the only way to get through the Christmas season—a technique she'd been practicing for months.

She got up from the couch, went to her computer and booted it up, waiting, staring into the middle distance. She'd already finished her spring and summer ordering, but there was always something to do. She could review invoices and e-mail. Anything to keep her mind distracted and active.

As she read her e-mails, a low rumble shook the computer. The flat-screen color monitor flashed then went dark. Jennifer sank, troubled.

"Oh no, not a hard disk crash!"

A low eerie moan emanating from inside the computer startled her. The room slowly filled with it—a deafening and frightening groan. It was the sound of loneliness, like a cold howling wind. Jennifer sprang back, afraid the computer might blow up. She looked on, astonished, as the monitor exploded into flashes of lightning, shooting out beams of blue and golden light that blinded her. She threw up her hand to cover her eyes.

Then, suddenly, the screen went black and silent. Jennifer slowly uncovered her face, eyes squinting. She heard bells, the same bells she'd heard in the shop earlier in the evening. They sounded like tiny wind chimes.

She studied the dark monitor, mystified. And then, as if emerging from a smoky fog, a face slowly began to materialize. Jennifer watched in wonder as the face gradually solidified: first the vague outline of a chin, then a nose, then a full mouth. Finally, cheeks, eyes, a forehead, and hair. When it was fully drawn, Jennifer gazed at a kindly-looking elderly woman with white hair done up in a bun, a bright smile and blinking, spirited eyes. Intrigued, Jennifer nosed forward. When the woman smiled, Jennifer retreated a little. The mouth opened and spoke in a digitized voice. "Hi, Jennifer!"

Jennifer pushed back from the desk. The woman began to sing.

"*We wish you a merry Christmas, we wish you a merry Christmas, we wish you a merry Christmas and a happy New Year!*"

Jennifer uttered a nervous laugh. "Who sent this silly electronic Christmas card?"

The woman kept singing. Jennifer slapped at the keyboard, struggling to shut the thing off—to shut it down—but with no success. Frustrated, she punched the ON/OFF button, but that didn't work either. By the time she reached down to flip off the power strip, the song finished. The woman smiled and waved. "Merry Christmas, Jennifer!"

The face faded and slowly dissolved.

Jennifer stood and began to pace, staring nervously at the glowing blue monitor. Finally, cautiously, she returned to the computer, wrote in her e-mail address, and waited to see what would happen. Everything seemed normal, so she answered some e-mails, bcc'ing herself to see if they went through. When they did, she started studying her suppliers' websites, ordering Valentine's Day and Easter merchandise.

Finally exhausted, she scrunched down into her favorite recliner and tried to sleep. It was impossible. Memories filled her mind with useless agitation.

Fighting anger, she pushed out of her chair, reached for her blue ski jacket and stepped outside onto the front deck. The air was cold and still; a light snow was still falling across the hushed countryside. Her eyes wandered the shadows made by evergreen trees, which dotted the rolling white hills. It was peaceful and beautiful, but she felt neither.

How would she survive the next month? Christmas Eve would be the biggest challenge. She'd work until 10 o'clock. There'd be plenty of late shoppers. She'd let Angela go at 6, but she'd stay. Christmas Eve night, she'd work on her website. If she made it through the night, then she'd stay in bed and read on Christmas Day.

She brushed snow off the deck railing. December 24$^{th}$. How cruel life had been to her. Two years ago, her father had a heart attack on December 24$^{th}$. Because her mother had died of cancer six years earlier, it was her next-door neighbor who'd called to tell her. He'd died quickly.

A year ago, on December 24$^{th}$, Lance had been killed

in a car accident on his way to meet her for their wedding rehearsal.

Jennifer closed her eyes, struggling not to relive the pain. "Lance!" she whispered. Lance, her childhood sweetheart; her high school sweetheart. Lance, whom she'd loved since she was 10 years old. They'd planned their wedding even then, and they'd never stopped loving each other. Everyone had said that their relationship was a gift from God, and she'd believed it, because her love for Lance was what kept her breathing, working and believing that she could somehow survive this life. Whenever he kissed her or told her how beautiful she was, she felt stronger. And she liked the fact that she didn't hear bells or see birds flying overhead or feel obsessed and out-of-control. It was a real love—grounded in the real world. Not head-over-heels in love, not rash or sappy. It was simple: he was there for her.

Lance was her best friend, the one person she could always trust, talk to and lean on. He was unassuming, unaware of his delectable good looks, even when attractive women eyed him desirably as they passed. Lance, who had so many friends, because he was such a good friend. Lance, who was going to be a pediatrician.

When she heard the news that he was dead, it seemed impossible to her. Death simply didn't exist for Lance. It wasn't an option. Lance could never just disappear into death. His life, his spirit, his breath were a part of her and always would be. How could anyone that vital, essential and indispensable just vanish into nothingness, where people spoke about him in the past; where memory failed to remember the entire truth of him, or the essential facts of a phrase he'd once uttered, or the movement of his arm, or the way he slept so soundly, even with the TV blaring.

His death had seemed unnatural, as if someone had told her that the sun had stopped giving heat or that flowers had lost their color and scent. She couldn't and wouldn't accept it. Until the funeral. Then, the unnatural became reality. Nothingness became emptiness. She fell into sickness, a debilitating illness that sent her to bed for days in rage and tears, into her own kind of death. She didn't know how to let him go.

Days later, her therapist chattered and stared at her like a dead fish. It all sounded like static to her—like so much babble.

Then on a drowning day, she'd managed to come up for air, abruptly deciding to leave town. To start over. Somewhere. Anywhere. She couldn't be in the same town where they had grown up together, gone to elementary school, junior high and high school together. The restaurants, shops and movie theaters all seemed painfully somber and empty, as if some great disaster had happened and only she realized it.

The sad faces of her friends disgusted her—the minister's comforting words angered her and she wanted no part of anyone's philosophy on why such things happen. Intellectually, she knew that this kind of thing had happened to others—many worse things had happened to others—but none of that mattered. Her world had been shattered beyond repair, and she knew that in order to survive, she would have to leave her hometown, forever, to try to find a new home.

That new home turned out to be Willowbury. She had first discovered it on the Internet. The shop was for sale. She had inherited some money when her father died and she'd received a small business loan.

Chilled to the bone, she slipped back inside, lit a fire in

the fireplace and crouched down next to it, staring vacantly. She could feel herself contract a little more inside. She was retreating back into her little cave, crawling toward the center of it, where she could protect herself from the outside world, filled with its slow dull pain and awful, fickle realities.

She gazed into the jagged flames, watching the logs shift, hearing the crackle and hiss of the wood. Slowly, she eased down next to the fire, feeling the heat of it, beginning another battle with the unseen enemies of her thoughts. She closed her eyes, and it was almost as if she could see the accusing red eyes of her thoughts looking back at her, sensing her vulnerability. They were awful, guilty thoughts, with the sharp teeth of rodents, waiting for her to relax enough for them to pounce and tear her to pieces.

She shut her eyes and, again, offered a silent plea for help.

# CHAPTER 3

It was December 22nd, and it was snowing again; a steady, quiet snowfall, devoid of the sharp chill that usually sailed down from Canada. A heavy accumulation was forecasted.

Frances Wintergreen, a white-haired woman with playful blue eyes that sparkled with wonder, sat perched behind the wheel of her candy-apple-red 1957 Ford Fairlane, peering through the windshield at the slapping windshield wipers. She took in the scenery as she drove along Collier's Road toward Willowbury. She had a date with Jennifer Taylor and, snowfall or not, she'd have to keep it.

Frances thought the scenes before her were reminiscent of Courier and Ives Christmas cards, complete with tall pines air-brushed by snow; horse-drawn sleighs galloping across the elegant countryside; and fat snowmen poised on the rolling white hills, with stove pipe hats, stick arms and shiny black eyes.

A white church steeple appeared, as she drove slowly through a red covered bridge that spanned Cutter's narrow bubbling stream. The road then unraveled past quaint Victorian homes and a few clumps of modern townhouses and condominiums, all nestled comfortably behind majestic firs and pines.

The road arched around Harvey's Pond, and Frances smiled when she saw ice skaters glide and twirl, some with precision and grace, others with reaching arms and scattering, falling bodies. It was all unfolding to the music of Christmas, because Harvey Trudeau taught music at the local high school and, many Christmases ago, he'd wired the speakers from his home.

Just beyond the Pond, on Morris Pike's Hill, kids struggled to the top, hauling sleds and snow tubes. They skidded down the slopes, squealing with delight as they skimmed across the glistening white carpet of newly fallen snow under a porcelain blue-gray sky.

As she approached Main Street, she smiled at the decorations. Hanging along side the stoplights were long, elegant icicles, swinging in an easy breeze. In the Village Green stood bold-eyed drummer boys with red and black uniforms, drum sticks raised and red hats poised. They seemed alive. A manger scene adorned the Methodist churchyard lawn, along with tall Victorian plastic carolers making silent music, their mouths formed in dramatic Os.

In the square, 5-foot-high candy canes blinked erratically to the tinny sound of *Jingle Bells*. Three angelic trumpeters surrounded the 20-foot evergreen tree that blazed with colored lights. It leaned precariously left, because of the thickening snow.

Mrs. Wintergreen continued on, watching children build a snowman, some pausing to sling snowballs and play catch.

Above her, a red and green plastic banner, stretched from one side of the street to the other, announced the yearly Christmas Festival and Parade on December $24^{th}$.

Shoppers hurried across the streets into shops and

markets, shopping bags and children in tow. Mrs. Wintergreen smiled and waved as she drove by on her way to Cards N' Stuff.

She found a parking spot nearby, parallel parked expertly and stepped out. The car drew curious eyes. Even partially covered with a layer of snow, one could see that it was a beauty—one you didn't see every day—kind of like Mrs. Wintergreen.

A man approached, looking it over, hands behind his back. "You've really got something there... What's the engine?"

Mrs. Wintergreen smiled proudly. "292 V8, automatic transmission. But it doesn't have power steering."

"Your husband restore it?"

Mrs. Wintergreen scolded him with her eyes. "No... I did! I did it completely by myself! And, I've done others as well."

He nodded, dubiously, looking first at the car and then back at Mrs. Wintergreen. "Remarkable."

"I'm glad you approve."

She was dressed in a full-length bright red coat, with a white collar and trim, heavy black snow boots and red mittens. Her apple-cheeks added a wholesome look.

The admiring man strolled away, but glanced back one last time, as if trying to remember something.

There was a comfortable familiarity about Mrs. Wintergreen that one couldn't easily understand, and when people passed, they often turned and smiled before moving on, as if they had known her for years. But then almost immediately, they hesitated, glanced back, and tried to remember where they'd last seen her. Surely she was someone's grandmother, who hadn't been to town in a while or, perhaps, she was a volunteer who had come to town to help bake cookies, candies and fudge for the Christmas Festival. Her expression was kind and wise, like someone who knew the world well and loved it passionately—unconditionally—in all of its mystery, adventure and pain.

Mrs. Wintergreen waved to everyone as she approached Cards N' Stuff and paused to stroke the arched back of Tippy Toe, the tan and white cat who lived at the firehouse up the street.

As usual, the shop was boiling with energy and excitement. Mrs. Wintergreen entered and stamped the snow off her boots onto the black plastic welcome mat. She could barely nudge her way in. The ringing doorbell brought a smile as she closed it quietly, allowing two sturdy women to muscle by. Reaching for one of the three-inch tall Santa Claus dolls, the first woman exclaimed, "They are so adorable!"

"Absolutely fabulous!" the second woman answered.

"And so reasonably priced. I just love Jennifer Taylor's taste," the first woman said.

Mrs. Wintergreen spotted Jennifer on a footstool, reaching for a jewelry box. Standing below her was an impatient, heavy-set woman, who couldn't seem to make up her mind.

"No, not that one! What is the matter with you?! I want the one next to the gold one!"

This was Agnes Stanton. She was a slow, somber woman in her middle '60s, who often carried several chips on her narrow shoulders and an impatient glare in her silvery eyes. She was the wealthiest person in town and famous for letting everyone know it. Her sharp tongue was legendary, and everyone feared it. No one, including Reverend Talbot, was exempt from its sting.

Agnes Stanton's bulky, black woolen coat was designed to hide girth, and it was largely successful. She wore a white, wide-brimmed hat for dramatic flair, and to ensure that she'd be noticed, catered to and, in her own words, "indulged."

Jennifer was doing her best to notice, cater to and indulge. On a foot stool, she struggled to grasp a golden jewelry box located on a top shelf. She reached, stretched, teetered and grabbed. Successful, she stepped down and presented it to Mrs. Stanton, who hastily opened the lid. It played *Jingle Bells.* Mrs. Stanton made an ugly face and slammed the lid closed. Shoppers turned toward the sound to see Mrs. Stanton give Jennifer a withering glare.

"I hate the song, and I despise the style of this box!" Mrs. Stanton snapped, thrusting the box back at Jennifer, as if it were a smelly piece of old garbage. "Your choice of products leaves much to be desired, young woman! And while I'm at it, please don't let your garbage cans spill over in the alleyway on garbage pickup day! They are an unhealthy eyesore and their presence shows that you have careless and indiscriminate habits."

With a climactic flourish, Mrs. Stanton whirled and shoved her way through the crowd and out the front door.

Jennifer struggled to contain her anger, as she stepped up to replace the box.

Mrs. Wintergreen slowly worked her way through the narrow aisle until she was only a few feet from Jennifer. She lifted a gentle hand, trying to get Jennifer's attention. Jennifer noticed.

"I'll be right with you," Jennifer said, stepping down.

Just then, a hulking man with a mild panic in his eyes seized Jennifer's shoulder. "I need to get a gift for my wife. Somebody down the street said you'd be able to help."

Jennifer gave Mrs. Wintergreen an apologetic glance. Mrs. Wintergreen nodded understandingly, and browsed the shelves and displays as Jennifer made suggestions to the nervous man.

A few moments later, Jennifer approached, looking at Mrs. Wintergreen curiously. "Have we met?"

"Not directly, my dear."

"You look very familiar to me."

"I hear that a lot. I suppose I have a familiar face," Mrs. Wintergreen said.

Jennifer studied it. "Have you ever been to Tennessee?"

"Oh yes, Jennifer, I have. A delightful state, filled with wonderful people."

"Oneida, Tennessee?"

"I've been through it, yes, although it's been many years."

"Maybe that's where I saw you," Jennifer said, satisfied for the moment. "What can I help you with?"

Mrs. Wintergreen looked around the busy shop. "I'm afraid I caught you at a bad time, my dear. I apologize."

"It's okay. That's why I'm here, to help you," Jennifer said, with a steely, efficient manner.

"I want to talk to you about something. By the way, I love those Santa Claus dolls."

Jennifer frowned. "Those things?" Then she caught herself and forced a smile in a mock spirited tone. "Oh, yes! A lot of people seem to like them. They're selling well. You were saying that you needed to talk to me about something?"

Both women were jostled and bumped as they stood in the crowded thoroughfare. Mrs. Wintergreen pointed to the back of the store where it was more secluded.

"Perhaps we could speak back there."

Jennifer hesitated, seeing Angela feverishly at work behind the cash register, and a line of people waiting. "You'll have to make this quick, ma'am."

"Yes, indeed," Mrs. Wintergreen said.

They managed to edge their way to the rear of the store, near the Christmas tree, where the CD player was. Natalie Cole was singing *O Tannenbaum.* Mrs. Wintergreen paused to softly sing along and conduct with her right hand.

*"Du grunst nich nur zur Sommerzeit."* [You are green in summertime.] *"Nein auch im winter, wenn es schneit."* [Also in winter, when it snows.]

She looked at Jennifer, beaming. "Pardon me. I love that song and she sings it so beautifully, don't you think?"

Jennifer controlled her mounting impatience. "Oh yes," she said, without sincerity.

Mrs. Wintergreen gathered herself, folding her hands and lifting her warm eyes toward Jennifer. "Jennifer… I have a gift for you."

Jennifer slanted her a suspicious look. "A gift… for me?"

"Yes."

"Okay…" Jennifer said, waiting, her alert eyes darting about the shop.

"It is Christmas after all, the time for gift-giving, for granting wishes," Mrs. Wintergreen continued.

"…What did you say your name is?"

"Mrs. Wintergreen."

"Mrs. Wintergreen, I appreciate the offer, but you don't really have to give me anything."

"Oh, but I want to, my dear."

"Okay. Can you give it to me now or do I have to go somewhere and pick it up?"

"You do indeed have to travel somewhere."

"Okay, and, where will I have to travel?" Jennifer asked, folding her arms tightly, obviously not interested.

Mrs. Wintergreen's voice rose in excitement. "Well, let's just say that it involves an adventure."

Jennifer dropped her head, then slowly lifted it again. Her arms fell to her sides. "I'm going to have to cut this short. I really do have to get back to work. Thank you for coming in. If you need anything at all, please let me know. Excuse me."

Jennifer rushed away toward the cash register to help Angela. Mrs. Wintergreen turned, lifted a disappointed eyebrow, and moved through the crowds toward the front door. As she passed through it, Jennifer craned her neck, watching her. To get a better look, she moved toward the front window and stared as inconspicuously as possible, as Mrs. Wintergreen climbed into her car and drove away.

At 6:30 that evening, Jennifer still hadn't decided what she was going to wear to the Hartmans' Christmas party. She'd tried on dress after dress and paraded before the mirror so many times that she couldn't tell any more what looked good and what didn't. Her hips looked too broad in the red dress; the white and royal blue was out of style; the gold strapless was too provocative; the cream and tan made her look pale and washed out; the light green with slender straps looked like she was trying too hard. The black designer dress that she'd paid a fortune for over a year ago brought the pain of memory. It was the last dress Lance had seen her in.

What did that leave her with? The pale blue, with

puffy shoulders and a plunging neckline. It showed cleavage. All wrong. And then there was a question of jewelry. She'd never felt comfortable wearing jewelry.

She was about to reach for the telephone to call the Hartmans, to tell them she wouldn't be able to make it, when the telephone rang. She answered it.

"Hello?"

"Hello, Jennifer. It's Mrs. Wintergreen. How are you?"

Jennifer closed her eyes, massaging the bridge of her nose. "I'm fine. What can I do for you?"

"I'm calling to see if you're going to the Hartmans' Christmas party."

"Actually, something has come…"

Mrs. Wintergreen interrupted. "… Excuse me for interrupting, my dear, I just want to say that, well…they're such delightful people and I know they would appreciate your being at their party. They think very highly of you."

Jennifer's eyes opened and she eased down into the closest chair. "I suppose you'll be there?"

Her voice was filled with a contagious enthusiasm. "Oh, yes, Jennifer! I wouldn't miss it for anything. And, by the way, I would still like to offer you that Christmas present. So I do hope we'll see you there, my dear."

Jennifer breathed out a sigh. "Yes, I'll be there."

After Jennifer hung up, she went into the bathroom and quickly brushed out her hair, applied mousse then screwed up her lips, discouraged. What she needed was a Christmas beauty angel. She quickly applied makeup, glancing nervously at her digital clock and realizing that she was going to be late.

In the bedroom, she ignored the rejected dresses lying in a rumpled pile on the bed, and hurried to her walk-in closet. She reached for her favorite pair of dark pants. Next she grabbed a red silk blouse and white ski sweater on the shelf above. The outfit would have to do.

From her red velvet jewelry box, she lifted the lid and closed her eyes. It played *Winter Wonderland.* Her mother had given it to her for Christmas many years ago. She reached in and made a random selection. When she opened her eyes she gasped. They were her least favorite earrings. Silver dangling icicles with a little diamond drip. She shrugged and fastened them on. An old gift from somebody—she couldn't remember. She resisted the temptation to pass by the mirror before snatching her coat and leaving the condo.

Driving through the snow-cleared streets, past houses sprinkled with Christmas lights, electric candles in the windows and plastic glowing snowmen waving and grinning, Jennifer felt a mild panic. She'd never been particularly comfortable in large groups. She was always afraid that she would disappoint somehow—say the wrong thing at the wrong time—do something so outrageous that she would wind up on the front page of the morning papers and be run out of town, humiliated and ostracized. It's why she was comfortable with numbers and spreadsheets. They were a constant. Numbers never lie. They give you back exactly what you put out and you can always count on 2 + 2 equaling 4.

She turned her light blue Mazda onto Shepherd Lane and stopped. It was a quiet, narrow street, embroidered by tall bare trees and inky shadows. It was also where the Hartmans lived. She nudged the car forward and ventured a look down the road, where only one home was visible, and it was lit up for Christmas. It was a massive

Tudor-style home, with a brick wall separating its broad snow-covered lawn from the street. White lights were strung on every eave and bush and along the top of the wall. The perimeter hedges and bare oaks and pines were wrapped in colored lights. Blue floodlights illuminated a manger scene and a 50s-style plastic Santa, complete with sleigh and reindeer.

Across the street from the house was an empty lot filled with cars, obviously being used as the parking lot for guests.

Jennifer shook her head and drove toward the house. She turned into the circular drive and stopped the car near the front door of the Hartman home. A high school kid dressed in a bright yellow parka, with stiff hair and active eyes, handed Jennifer a ticket as she climbed out, feeling the sharp chill of the wind. He slid behind the wheel, closed the door and shot away from the driveway across the road to the parking lot.

She turned toward the house, hearing lively music coming from inside, recognizing the song as *Jingle Bell Rock*. Mustering courage, she approached the front door, noticing the large Christmas wreath with a bright red bow above the knocker. She found a doorbell and pressed it.

A moment later, the door opened and a silver-haired man dressed in a tuxedo, with a red silk scarf artfully arranged and blooming from his jacket pocket, welcomed her with a pleasant smile. The smells of pine and turkey filled her nose.

She presented him with her invitation and he led her into the roomy foyer framed in white lights, garlands and holly. He took her coat, passing it to a young beauty dressed in red velvet, and then escorted Jennifer to the party.

They entered a spacious and grandly decorated two-level room, where Christmas seemed to leap out at her from every corner. The four-piece band burst into song, *Rocking around the Christmas Tree*, and the room sprang to life with dancing and clapping.

People were gathered in groups, conversing, laughing, drinking or standing near the band, rocking to the music. Waiters and waitresses, dressed in black and white with red bow ties, carefully meandered through the crowds, offering drinks and hors d'oeuvres.

The women wore magnificently stylish dresses of green, red, black and gold, with bows, gold jewelry and artful hairdos. The men wore white shirts with Christmas ties, red and green cashmere sweaters or dark suits and open-collared red or green shirts. Jennifer swallowed away nerves as she looked around.

Poinsettias were everywhere, surrounding the band and on the mantel, windowsills and side tables. A towering spruce, decorated with red ornaments and white lights, stood 10 feet from the glowing masonry fireplace, where five-foot Nutcrackers stood at attention on either side. Children hopped and played, dazzled by the spectacle and cheerful energy.

Jennifer noticed baskets of presents, lavishly wrapped, placed around the room and near the red and green skirted table, where food was being arranged for the buffet. The table itself was embellished with a swag of greenery, Victorian-style ornaments, pinecones and candy canes.

The atmosphere was charged with celebration, expectation and possibility, but Jennifer found it all overwhelming. She was thankful that no one had noticed her. She tucked her head, spun around and walked briskly to the front door. The coat check girl looked confused when

Jennifer dropped a dollar in the tip jar and asked for her coat. The butler, too, examined her quizzically as he opened the door for her.

"I'm sorry, I have the wrong house," Jennifer said, exiting.

She descended the stairs and waved for the parking attendant. He hurried over, puzzled when she asked for her car.

Mrs. Wintergreen had been watching Jennifer, curiously, while munching a Christmas cookie and sipping eggnog. She saw Jennifer leave. Taking two sugar cookies along with her, she followed.

# CHAPTER 4

Jennifer stood at the foot of the stairs, waiting anxiously for the car attendant to fetch her car, regretting her decision to come. She felt exposed and vulnerable. She didn't belong with those people—with any people. She wanted to be alone.

A brand-new dark SUV rolled into the circular driveway and stopped at the edge of the walkway, where she was standing.

Richard Steady, her insurance agent, sprang out. Jennifer cringed. She'd almost escaped without seeing anyone. Richard was a talker.

"Hi there, Jennifer," he said, all bubbly and smiles.

Richard was shorter than Jennifer. He was stocky and square, dressed in his usual dark suit, red business tie and cashmere overcoat. His dark eyes were earnest; his thin, arching eyebrows raised; his voice always low and instructive, as if he were teaching a seminar.

"Snow, snow and more snow is what they're forecasting," he said rubbing his leather gloved hands together.

A second attendant, loose-limbed and anxious, hurried over and took Richard's car keys. He dropped behind the wheel, slammed the door and raced away.

"You coming or going?" Richard asked, his breath

puffing white gusts of vapor.

"I'm…I have to leave. You know, business things."

At 42, married and childless, it seemed that Richard played the role of father to nearly everyone in town, offering advice on everything from dating to hair styles to diets. Many people felt that Richard was more of a father confessor than the local priest, Father Abernathy, the only problem being that during the course of listening to one's confession, Richard was apt to, and indeed often did, try to sell one an insurance policy.

"How's the party?" Richard asked.

"Nice…real nice…festive," Jennifer said, standing on tiptoes, looking for her car.

"How's your business doing?" Richard asked.

"Incredibly busy."

Richard gave her one of his fatherly looks. "Have you been getting to know any of the young men in our town, Jennifer?"

"I've been busy."

"All work and no play is not good, Jennifer. You must have balance in your life. Balanced relationships, balanced diet and balanced work habits. These are all very important for a truly happy life. It's the key to everything."

"How is your wife?" Jennifer asked, quickly changing the subject.

"Oh, Molly is fine. Probably in the Hartman kitchen, getting in everyone's way. But she just loves Christmas. She helped decorate the place. Hope it looks good. What do you think?"

"Yes. Looks real…well like Christmas."

Richard clasped his hands at his waist, shaking his head a little as a preamble to a serious subject. "Jennifer,

I've been meaning to come by and talk to you about your insurance coverage. I was looking over your policy the other day and I'm a little concerned that you may not have all the coverage you need."

"That's nice of you, Richard, but I think I'm in pretty good shape right now."

"Freezing temperatures, blustery winds, ice, sleet and snow can cause severe damage to your building and property, Jennifer. Consider the blizzard of 2009, which was the fifth most costly in the history of the United States. Did you know that?"

"No, Richard, I didn't."

"It caused an estimated $1.75 billion in damage."

"That much?"

"Yes, that much. And then there was the storm of the century in 1993. Northern locations, like ours, are most likely to be hard-hit on a regular basis, so don't underestimate our winter storms. I know you're from Tennessee where you get the occasional storm, but nothing like the kind of devastating storm that can strike us."

"So you want me to expand my policy, Richard?"

"Well, let's consider it. Frozen pipes can cause a lot of damage, not to mention collapsed roofs due to the weight of snow, and interior water seepage due to blocked roof drains. Now, I know you're a good business woman—an excellent business woman— and I respect that, I really do, so I think you should expand your policy to cover all the items I just mentioned."

Jennifer thought it over for a moment. "Everyone says that January and February are the worst months for storms around here."

Richard nodded. "That's correct," he said, suddenly distracted by an approaching limousine.

Jennifer followed his gaze. "Why don't you come by

after Christmas and we'll discuss it."

Richard brightened. "Wise, Jennifer. A very wise decision."

The limousine drew up and stopped. The driver climbed out, circled around the back to the passenger door, and opened it.

Agnes Stanton emerged, slowly, surveying the area with a disapproving expression and a mumbled misery that no one could understand and didn't wish to.

Jennifer whispered to Richard under her breath. "Don't leave. She's always coming into the shop and bawling me out for something."

Richard whispered, "She was almost tolerable until her husband died. Now, she's a nightmare." Then as an afterthought, because he was concerned about his business image, "...But God bless her, Jennifer. God just bless her!"

Jennifer stared, doubtingly. "Yeah... right."

They could hear the band frolicking through *Frosty the Snow Man* when Mrs. Stanton waddled over.

"Merry Christmas," Jennifer and Richard said, affably.

She looked at Richard, with cool laser eyes, and just as he was about to initiate conversation, she threw up her broad hand, like a stop sign. "Don't start with me, Richard Steady. I have all the insurance I'm ever going to get, on all my properties, cars and relatives, and on every limb of my body. I don't want information, I don't want advice, and I definitely do not want to be asked for any further referrals to any of my friends, whom you haven't already pestered, perturbed or perplexed. Do not assume that just because this is the season of giving and goodwill, that I am willing to give you anything, now, or at any time in the foreseeable future."

Richard didn't blink or blanch. He ginned, genuinely, as if the full force of her insulting tone and acerbic words bounced off him like a BB off tin.

"Well, if you ever need anything at all, you just call me, day or night, and I'll make sure that you're taken care of, Mrs. Stanton. Are you going to taste the Hartmans' famous eggnog?" Richard asked.

"Never touch the stuff! Way too fattening!"

"Only once a year," he coaxed, lifting his eyebrows playfully, like Groucho.

"Don't be patronizing, Richard."

Richard shrugged, turned and retreated toward the house, while Jennifer watched him, feeling forsaken and jittery.

Mrs. Stanton rolled her eyes, exasperated. "The man is insufferable!" she snapped.

Jennifer finally saw her own car advancing through the parking lot. It wouldn't be long now.

Mrs. Stanton turned her steely eyes to Jennifer. "Ms. Taylor, I'm disappointed in you! I am an early riser and always have been. I leave my house for my morning walk, which, as you know, is on Lincoln Street, at precisely 6:20. I pass by your card shop at 6:30. In the last two weeks, because it has snowed, I have nearly fallen twice in front of your shop. Your sidewalk has not been cleared of snow. It's outrageous! It's dangerous and it's a hazard! If I ever do fall and break an ankle or a hip, I will prosecute you to the fullest extent of the law!"

Jennifer took a step backwards. "Mrs. Stanton, I've hired one of the local high school boys to shovel the walk, but he doesn't get there until 7:30 in the morning."

Mrs. Stanton shook a threatening finger at her. "You've heard my warning, Ms. Taylor. If I were you, I'd heed it and take the necessary action."

Jennifer shoved her hands into her coat pockets and began rocking impatiently on her heels.

Mrs. Stanton regarded her critically. "Are you leaving the party so soon, Ms. Taylor? Why it can't be later than 7:30."

Jennifer watched as her car stopped in the middle of the road, beside Richard's SUV. The attendants were having an unhurried conversation. She wanted to scream. "Yes, I'm afraid I have some work to do," Jennifer said, ignoring her.

"You can't have stayed long at the party, not that I blame you. But what will people think? It doesn't make a good impression, to leave so soon. Being new to this town and in business for yourself, you should want to make a good impression, Ms. Taylor, and I'm afraid this action runs contrary to that. I admit that J. D. Hartman can be a crashing bore and a big blowhard, but that doesn't excuse you for your bad manners."

Finally Jennifer's car arrived. "Thank you, Mrs. Stanton; I'll keep it in mind."

"You'd better do more than just keep it in mind! Once you make enemies in Willowbury, you'd better just lock your door and leave town!"

Jennifer slipped the attendant a dollar, and slithered behind the wheel of her car, closing the door in Mrs. Stanton's starched and insulted face.

As she drove away and glanced at the rearview mirror, Jennifer caught sight of Mrs. Stanton staring at the fleeing car, her hands stuck on her bulging hips.

Back on the main highway, heavy flecks of snow crashed into her windshield, fell thickly across the shaft of her headlights and covered the road. Jennifer didn't slow down. She kept the car plunging through the night. She shuddered, happy to have escaped the party and all those silly people, with their silly little Christmas outfits, frivolous Christmas jewelry and bogus Christmas spirit. Christmas spirit! What spirit? When you analyzed it in the full light of truth and didn't "cook the books," so to speak, you could easily see that their spirit was nothing more than self-aggrandizement.

The mayor and his wife were just playing politics. Richard Steady was there because it was good business and he might sell another policy while he sipped eggnog or danced or lingered under the mistletoe with some nasty widow like Mrs. Stanton. Speaking of Mrs. Stanton, her reason for coming to the party was obvious. Everyone there would bow down to her, even though she'd insult most of them one way or the other. She was certainly disliked, or even despised, by everyone in town, but who was going to turn their back on power and wealth?

The band was there because they were being paid to be there, as were the caterers and waiters and waitresses. She didn't remember seeing any of them with happy faces.

As for the rest of the people, they got their chance to inflate their egos, rub shoulders with the influential and popular, and get free food and drinks in the process. More power to them.

As she approached Harvey's Pond, Jennifer felt a sinking feeling in her chest. She didn't want to go back to her lonely apartment, afraid that old Christmas memories would begin to close in on her from every corner.

She suddenly remembered that she had her ice skates with her! Jennifer had only been skating for a couple of weeks now. She'd never learned how to skate in Tennessee, but Willowbury had so many beautiful ponds, and ice-skating was such a large part of the culture, that Angela had finally talked her into it. Jennifer used to roller blade in Tennessee, so she didn't think she needed lessons. Instead, she was trying to teach herself whenever she found the time. She was in desperate need of a distraction.

When Jennifer spotted the dark and narrow virgin snow-covered road, she took the turn a little too fast and the back wheels of the car skidded sharply to the left. She quickly recovered, spinning the wheel left gently and applying the brakes. After taking a little breath, she continued on, passing stately pines, newly sugar-coated with snow, until she finally arrived at a little wooden gazebo. No one else was there. One yellow spotlight atop the gazebo bathed the ice-covered pond. She parked and turned off the engine, listening to the deep silence. Finally, she got out and stepped around to the trunk to retrieve her ice skates. She trudged through the squeaky snow until she arrived at the gazebo, happy there wasn't any Christmas music playing. After slapping away snow from the wooden bench, she sat and laced up her skates. She looked around, feeling oddly heavy and out of place—not a part of the excruciatingly beautiful scene around her, a snow globe of tranquility and wonder. How was it possible, she thought, to feel like an alien—like a refugee without roots, without a home, without a beating heart—among such beauty?

She stood and gripped the wooden railing for a time, finding courage, and then ventured out, clumsily, onto the glistening ice that was covered with a thin layer of snow. She was already shivering from the frosty night air.

Her legs felt weak and shaky. Her breath came fast, in white puffs. She had the image of herself as an uncoordinated clown performing at a circus, scampering unsteadily across the ice, her jerky body lurching and bobbing, her hands reaching for an invisible support. It was a good thing no one was around to see her make a complete fool of herself.

She wobbled and skipped as she battled to stay upright. Her lungs began to burn from the cold. Halfway across the pond, she picked up dubious speed and then, suddenly, like an unlikely miracle, she hit her stride, finding the zone of tenuous balance and perilous freedom. It was wonderful! She was beginning to feel carefree. The wind across her face gave her a sense of elation, as she scraped a path across the ice, like someone seasoned and confident. If only someone could see her now, as she cruised the pond, like a woman in control, unhampered by doubt, suspicion and fear. If only she could hold the position forever, a person undaunted by the conspiring elements of sharp wind, slippery ice and corrupt balance. She wanted more. She lifted a shaky hand to try for some artistic form, to expand herself out, to fly like a swan across the ice.

That's when disaster struck. Her feet began to take on a life of their own. They deserted her and slid away in different directions, like two trains: one traveling east, the other west. She watched, horrified and helpless, knowing that a train wreck was imminent. Panic burned her throat. The trains jumped the tracks.

When she bounced on the ice, the breath burst from her lungs. She fell backwards and slid away in a clumsy and chaotic dance of flailing arms and legs, just like a turtle on its back, whizzing across the ice helpless and comical.

When she finally came to rest, cold and sore, she lay back flat, staring up at the dark moving sky, feeling the cool tickle of snowflakes on her face. She was isolated—

so very alone. God, how she missed Lance.

Suddenly, from out of nowhere, Mrs. Wintergreen's face cut into her vision, smiling down at her.

Startled, Jennifer blinked quickly, disoriented, trying to erase the image, sure it was an illusion. But Mrs. Wintergreen remained.

"Hello, Jennifer. You just took a pretty bad fall. Are you all right?"

Jennifer didn't move. "Where did you come from? There was no one around."

"I was around. I was watching you," Mrs. Wintergreen said, extending Jennifer her hand. "May I help you up?"

Jennifer eyed her warily. "I thought you said you were going to the Hartmans' Christmas party."

She nodded. "I was."

"I didn't see you."

"I saw you."

Jennifer took Mrs. Wintergreen's hand and allowed her to help her up.

"So you followed me?"

"Yes."

Jennifer massaged her right hip and grimaced in pain.

"Let me help you over to the gazebo," Mrs. Wintergreen said.

Jennifer nodded. Mrs. Wintergreen held her arm and skated alongside her until they arrived safely at the gazebo and sat down.

"Are you sure you're all right, my dear?" Mrs. Wintergreen asked.

"Yes, probably just bruised…nothing serious."

Jennifer looked at Mrs. Wintergreen's placid face, studied her alert eyes and saw a comfortable reliability and assurance in them. She noticed her clothes: a red and green ski cap, with embroidered reindeer and children; the woolen red scarf tied loosely around her neck, the burgundy sweater and Little Red Riding Hood cape over her shoulders, the emerald skirt and antique-looking ice skates, with sparkling runners.

"Who are you?"

"Someone who wants to give you a Christmas gift."

"No," Jennifer said, abruptly, "I mean, who are you, really, and where do you come from? I've never seen you around town before, I mean until the other day in my shop."

"Well..., Jennifer, people often look at me strangely when I tell them who I really am. So I don't tell them."

"I'm looking at you strangely now. It's more than a little strange when someone follows you around like you've been following me."

Mrs. Wintergreen folded her hands in her lap and looked straight ahead. Just as she was about to speak, Jennifer said, "And don't tell me you're some kind of Christmas angel!"

"Oh, no! Although I wanted to be when I was a little girl."

"So?"

"Well, I'm what you might call... a kind of Christmas Spirit."

Jennifer nodded, rapidly, her eyes blinking rapidly. "Okay... okay..."

"It's difficult for some people to believe that we exist."

Jennifer narrowed her eyes. "Well I can't imagine why," she said, sarcastically.

"At Christmas, happiness, hope and love are needed the most, Jennifer. So, I, and others like me, come to help out from time to time."

Jennifer sighed and looked away. "I see. And where are you from?"

"Well, you could say I'm from right here. I mean, in a sense, I'm always here."

Jennifer shut her eyes in impatience. "Okay, let's not even go there. What did you say your name was?"

Mrs. Wintergreen leaned toward her. "I introduced myself to you earlier today, Jennifer, when I came to your shop. I'm Mrs. Frances Wintergreen."

"Well, that's a very cheery name. Wintergreen sounds very... holiday-ish, doesn't it?"

"Yes, Jennifer."

Jennifer looked away, irritated, watching the snow blow and drift. "Well, isn't that nice."

"Of course, you don't believe in me," Mrs. Wintergreen said, shrugging.

"No!" Jennifer said, emphatically. "No, I do not believe that you're some kind of Christmas Spirit. Forgive me, but I stopped believing in Santa Claus a long, long time ago," Jennifer said, lifting her hand and then dropping it helplessly in her lap. "Do you have family nearby or someone I could call, maybe a therapist, a hospital?"

Mrs. Wintergreen laughed. "You can see why I don't often tell people who I am, Jennifer. I almost always get the same response."

"Look, I would really appreciate it if you'd just leave me alone."

Mrs. Wintergreen looked deeply into Jennifer's eyes. "Jennifer, it was your request that brought me here. You're the one who asked for help, the day after Thanksgiving, remember?"

Jennifer shifted, anxiously. "Look, Mrs. Wintergreen, I don't want to be disrespectful, but I think this joke has gone on long enough. I do not believe that you are some incarnate Spirit of Christmas, and, unless you can show me some miracle, I'm going to ask you, very nicely, to stop following me."

Mrs. Wintergreen looked at Jennifer knowingly. "I've been watching you for some time, Jennifer. It was I who sang to you that night, when you were closing the shop. Remember? You thought it was coming from the CD player. You checked the CD player and it was turned off. That same night, at home, when you were working on your computer, I appeared on the screen. I sang to you again."

Mrs. Wintergreen began to sing "We wish you a merry Christmas, We wish you a merry Christmas, We wish you a merry Christmas and a happy New Year. Remember?"

Jennifer felt a prickle of heat shoot up her spine. She stared, alarmed. "Who are you?"

"I told you."

Jennifer's breath came fast. She swallowed. "That was an electronic Christmas card," she said, trying to convince herself. "People send those things all the time."

"I know. I sent it to you."

Jennifer shot up, forgetting she was still wearing ice skates. She wobbled, lost her balance and dropped back down. She studied Mrs. Wintergreen, speechless.

"I'm offering you a gift, an opportunity, Jennifer. It's your choice."

Jennifer turned away. "What are you talking about? What gift?"

"Well, I have always been known as the romantic in our family, and I have never apologized for it. Romantic adventures are one of the great joys of life."

Jennifer closed her eyes tightly, as if trying to shut Mrs. Wintergreen out. "Really. So, you're like the matchmaker of the Christmas Spirit family?"

"No. I don't match-make, but I can point you in a direction that you wouldn't normally take, either because you fear it or because you simply don't know that the opportunity exists. At Christmas, I have the good fortune to offer possibilities to those who are deserving, courageous and adventurous. This year, I have chosen you, Jennifer. I can offer you a wonderful Christmas adventure. But it is entirely your choice. You have to take the necessary steps to have the adventure."

Jennifer opened her eyes, avoiding Mrs. Wintergreen's. "The only adventure I want, Mrs. Wintergreen, is to be able to sleep late on Christmas morning."

Mrs. Wintergreen's face turned severe; her tone, somber and foreboding. "You're going to be tested soon, my dear. You'll have to make a choice anyway. I was hoping I could make it a little easier for you."

Jennifer crossed her arms, nervous. "What do you mean, tested?"

Frances stood. "Jennifer, when I look at you, I see a heavy belt of bitterness and anger wrapped around your chest, pulled tightly, constricting your breath, your life and the goodness of your heart."

"I feel fine."

"You need to move on with your life, Jennifer. If you don't… if you don't move on soon, it could be too late. Just like it was too late for Agnes Stanton."

Jennifer's eyes widened in recognition and fear. "What about Mrs. Stanton?"

"She was offered an opportunity many years ago. I offered it to her, but she refused it. I hope you won't refuse, Jennifer. The world needs people with good hearts, with open hearts, at Christmas and throughout the entire year."

Jennifer stiffened, fists clenched. "My heart is fine just as it is. As for Christmas… It's just a silly holiday."

"You're lost, Jennifer," Mrs. Wintergreen said.

Jennifer bristled. "I'm lost? No, not me, but I lost someone on Christmas—last Christmas Eve—someone who was loving, steady and joyful, who had a good and open heart, someone who would have helped the world and made it a better place. He was killed in a car accident! A pointless and senseless death! That's the kind of world we live in. The world of random violence, death and loss. Okay, fine, I accept it. Now, leave me alone!"

Jennifer averted Mrs. Wintergreen's eyes.

Mrs. Wintergreen remained still. "Wouldn't Lance want you to be happy, Jennifer?"

Jennifer shot her a startled glance. "How do you know his name? I didn't say his name."

"Like I said earlier, Jennifer, I've been watching you for a long time."

Jennifer shifted, uncomfortably. "I don't know who you are, Mrs. …, but I'm doing fine. I have a nice place to live and I have a successful business. That's enough for me."

"Is it really, Jennifer?"

"Yes!"

"To receive my gift, you'll have to leave town, tomorrow."

Jennifer laughed, harshly. "I couldn't leave town now even if I wanted to. It's impossible. This is the busiest time of year. I'm not going anywhere."

Frances Wintergreen stood. "All right, my dear… it's your choice. Goodbye. I do hope you find some peace in your life."

Mrs. Wintergreen walked her skates onto the ice,

leaned forward and glided away across the pond, disappearing into the scrim of falling snow.

Jennifer slowly struggled to her feet, straining her eyes to find Mrs. Wintergreen. But she was gone. Trembling and shaken, Jennifer slowly eased back down, staring longingly into the night.

# CHAPTER 5

That night, Jennifer slept fitfully. At five in the morning, she finally gave up, pushing out of bed, her throat dry, her chest heavy with grief; a ridiculous feeling of desperation brought beads of sweat to her forehead.

She went to the window and parted the gauze-like curtains, wiping her tired eyes and peering out. It was still snowing! Heavy flakes. The world was covered in mounds and cones of it, blowing wildly into drifts against her building. She could already hear the growl of a snow blower in the distance and the rhythmic scrape of a shovel. She folded her arms against her white flannel gown for warmth and slipped her feet into her brown fuzzy house shoes.

In the living room, she switched on the TV and flopped down in her chair. The handsome weatherman said that the snow would stop by mid morning, but the accumulation would be over 14 inches!

She made coffee and skipped breakfast. Jennifer used to love breakfast—it was her favorite meal—but she hadn't had much of an appetite in months.

After a shower, she dressed in a heavy brown turtleneck, jeans, and warm socks. She pulled on her brown rubber boots, grabbed her down coat and dashed out the front door. She needed to get to the shop before 6:30, shovel and salt the front walk, just in case Mrs. Stanton took her usual walk. It would be just like her to walk by the shop, in the middle of the snowstorm, just to spite her.

In the parking lot, it took 10 minutes to clear the front and back windshields of her car. When she glanced at her watch, she grimaced. It was almost six o'clock! She'd have to hurry. Jennifer opened the door, kicked the snow off her boots and got in.

The road into town had been cleared earlier in the night, but a new layer of snow made it treacherous and slow-going. Hers was the only car on the road, and it aggravated her to think that her life was being dictated by a bitter old woman who delighted in making everyone's life miserable, including her own.

It was almost 6:25 by the time Jennifer arrived on Main Street. The stores, cars and sidewalks were nearly smothered in blowing, glistening snow. Impatience and urgency made her press the accelerator with a firm foot. Finally, she saw Cards N' Stuff ahead. Surely, Mrs. Stanton wouldn't be out taking her normal walk. Not in this weather!

But just as Jennifer was approaching the shop, she spotted a lone figure, armed with a cane and leaning into the wind, trudging along like an old persevering pilgrim. Jennifer immediately recognized Mrs. Stanton, dressed in her heavy black coat and ostentatious white hat.

Jennifer cursed under her breath. Mrs. Stanton was no more than five feet from the front of Cards N' Stuff! Impulsively, Jennifer pressed forward, spotting her preferred parking place, near the alley.

Suddenly, everything seemed to happen at once, and in slow motion. Mrs. Stanton stepped in front of the shop, stabbing away at the snow with her cane.

Jennifer's back tires slid away into chaos. It was as if the world was spinning away from her. She frantically fought for control of the car, but the steering wheel became useless. She was slipping away toward the east wall of Cards N' Stuff. Jennifer held her breath.

Just then, Mrs. Stanton's left foot found an unfortunate old patch of ice beneath the newly fallen snow. She felt it give way, and her cane, which should have been a support, slipped from her hand and sailed away into a snowdrift. Jennifer watched in horror as Mrs. Stanton's body lifted from the earth and rose like a great bird above the spread of undulating snow. She seemed suspended in time. For a brief hopeful moment, Jennifer had the irrational belief that she could somehow scramble from her car and rescue Mrs. Stanton, as one would rescue a priceless fragile vase falling from a great height.

But there was no rescue. There was no one to catch Mrs. Stanton and there was no one to stop Jennifer's car from its collision course with the garbage cans in the alleyway, and the inevitable impact into the side of the building.

Mrs. Stanton's body finally hit the snow, like a massive meteorite striking the earth. The impact threw up a plume of whiteness. The crater was deep and impressive. Mrs. Stanton let out an almighty howl that scattered chirping sparrows into the trees. Her yell was eclipsed by Jennifer's car slamming into the garbage cans, and colliding into the side wall of Cards N' Stuff.

Then there was silence. But only a brief one.

From somewhere, close by, came a low rumble. It was a foreboding sound, like the low moan of fate in the apprehension of an imminent catastrophe.

Cards N' Stuff began to shimmy and quake. Icicles snapped and fell. Fractures formed on the roof. Sliding snow whooshed down in avalanches, crashing to the ground.

Mrs. Stanton was frozen in fear, looking bug-eyed, hearing a roar, like the sea.

Jennifer managed to shove open the jammed car door and roll out, falling into a mound of snow. She heard the frightening sound, struggled to her feet and staggered away from the building, running, stumbling and gasping.

There was a terrible, miserable groan as the roof buckled and plunged down into the shop in a storm of wood, roof-tiles, dirt and snow. In violent hammer-like blows, it shattered snow globes, jewelry boxes and porcelain figurines. It smashed glass displays and chopped through shelves, burying Christmas angels, Santa Clauses, Christmas cards and delicate earrings. The window Christmas displays were blown into oblivion; the Victorian town demolished; the electric train flicked away and buried by a powerful cascading shaft of dirt and ice. The family around the piano was pummeled and destroyed.

In a final act of destruction, sprinkler pipes ruptured, shooting streams of water into the air like geysers, flooding the place. Books, CDs and DVDs floated by, little boats navigating a chaotic space.

When it was finally over, an uneasy silence settled in, like a warning.

Jennifer lifted unsteadily to her feet, her mouth open in shock, her eyes wide and burning. She saw Mrs. Stanton. She was nearly buried in snow. Jennifer frantically rushed over, dropped to her knees beside the woman and began brushing snow off her coat, face and hair.

"Mrs. Stanton! Mrs. Stanton! Are you all right!?"

Mrs. Stanton was spitting snow from her mouth. Her arms were outstretched and waving; her face red, white and splotchy.

"Call an ambulance! Call the police! Call the fire department! And get the hell away from me! Just get the hell away from me! I'm going to prosecute you!"

Jennifer looked around, disoriented and blunted. She wanted to run, but she couldn't move or think. She reached for her cell phone and called an ambulance.

She walked toward the firehouse, aimlessly, only vaguely aware of the approaching sirens, which, like distant memories, seemed to be coming from a long way off. There was a strange cast to the world, of watercolor grays, salmons and blues and, suddenly, a limpid sky. The snow stopped.

She saw the faces of concerned paramedics and volunteer firemen as they rushed to the scene, helping Mrs. Stanton to a stretcher, darting about Cards N' Stuff, assessing the damage. Cars driving by stopped and people emerged, shocked, anxious to help.

Jennifer saw them, but somehow felt removed from the whole scene and, as she stood there watching, she saw shadowy images and indefinite shapes. Gradually, even they seemed to melt away—leaving a canvas of pure white, like a flat piece of blank white paper, where there was no particular definition or point of reference. If her heart was beating, she wasn't aware of it. She felt like a tree in winter. No obvious pulse, just bare, skinny limbs—dead-like—left to rattle in the cold wind.

She could have been standing there, in the street, for minutes or for hours, before the black Mercedes drew up to the curb and J. D. Hartman bounded out, quickly taking in the surroundings with a dramatic shake of his head. He started toward her in a rush of concern.

"Jennifer…!"

Jennifer kept staring at the collapsed building and hectic scene before her, lost in her nightmare. She watched as the ambulance carrying Mrs. Stanton drove away, siren screaming, red dome light sweeping the area.

"Jennifer! Jennifer, it's J. D. Hartman."

Jennifer became aware of a voice. She turned slowly toward it, allowing her eyes to finally focus on the Mayor's pinched face.

"Jennifer… are you all right?"

Jennifer nodded, dully.

In the next hour, Jennifer spoke with the police and then with Richard Steady, who was somber and apologetic, struggling for his usual optimism. There would be papers to fill out, forms to study, options to consider, but Jennifer couldn't deal with any right then. Finally, Mayor Hartman turned to her as they watched her car being towed to the garage, where Richard would appraise it more closely, and where it would eventually be repaired, sold or traded.

"Can I take you home?" the Mayor asked.

Jennifer noted the shattered headlights and crumpled right hood. Poor thing looked like it had been in a fight and lost, Jennifer thought. She'd really liked that car.

"I don't want to go home," Jennifer said.

"Then I'll take you to our house. Gladys will make some hot chocolate. You're shivering. You're going to catch pneumonia, if you don't get inside. Please."

Jennifer didn't respond. "I should be here. See if there's anything I can salvage."

"They're not going to let you go in there. It's too dangerous. There's nothing you can do, Jennifer. Nothing at all. Please, let me take you to our house."

Jennifer looked at him, sadly. "No… take me home... I just want to go home."

In the Mayor's car, Jennifer sat slumped and depressed. They traveled down the two-lane road toward her condominium and she stared out the window, drearily, as they passed Harvey's Pond. A small group of skaters edged across the ice, like sailboats, leaning into the wind.

"Did you have insurance?" the Mayor asked.

"Some. Not all I need. I was going to get more... next month."

The Mayor turned away in a fretful silence.

"I was just about to move into the black," Jennifer said, flatly. "Christmas sales were strong."

"That damned place is cursed!" the Mayor said, bitterly.

Jennifer turned to him. "Cursed? What do you mean?"

He shook his head quickly, wishing he hadn't spoken. "Nothing… just…"

"Mayor Hartman, tell me!"

"Two years ago, that building was a bookshop and café. It did so well and then… well, a tragic thing happened. The woman who leased it, Donna, died of leukemia. She was only 29 years old. I'm sure you've already heard the story."

"No..."

"...We were all very fond of Donna. She was married to my son, Alex."

"Your son? I didn't know you had a son."

"Gladys and I seldom speak about him. He and I didn't always get along very well, but I love him more than my own life. We got into so many damned arguments over the last few years. He hated my politics—disagreed with everything I stood for. Then, after Donna's death, Alex left town. Just kind of disappeared. He took his son, Jason, our only grandson, with him."

"How old was Jason?"

"He was 4 years old. The cutest and smartest little child," J. D. said, proudly. "I guess all grandparents say that, don't they? He's six now."

"Have you stayed in touch with your son?" Jennifer asked.

"He wrote occasionally, to his mother, but then he stopped writing altogether and we lost track of them. Gladys was so worried that she made me hire a private investigator to find them. They were eventually located in Kearney, Nebraska. Alex was working as a waiter in some restaurant."

The Mayor opened his mouth as if to finish his sentence, but then stopped. "He was a teacher, such a wonderful teacher. Taught history and sometimes literature at the high school. Anyway, we called him, but he didn't return our calls. We wrote him and begged him to come home or at least stay in contact with us, but he didn't, and we soon lost track of him again. We located him one other time in California, but again, after we contacted him, he didn't write or call. Finally, we stopped. Now, we just pray. What else can we do?"

Jennifer looked at the Mayor, saw the sorrow on his face, and noticed the light had left his eyes. "I'm sorry, Mayor. Life is so cruel, and I guess we all feel it more at this time of year, when we're fed all these sugary, impossible fantasies about peace on earth and love and joy."

The Mayor gave her a sideways glance, afraid to pull

his eyes from the road. When he spoke, his voice was steady, but Jennifer could hear the emotion in it. "We must believe in those things, Jennifer, otherwise we're just lost. We must try to find them and live them, otherwise what hope do we have?"

"Face it, Mayor, we're all lost. It's better to face it—to face the reality—than to believe in fantasies and illusions of peace on earth and goodwill toward men and women. That world just doesn't exist and never will exist. That's just not the way reality is."

J. D. Hartman looked at Jennifer compassionately. "You've had a tough blow, Jennifer. Get some rest and you'll feel better. We missed you at the Christmas party. I wish you'd have come."

Jennifer sighed. "I couldn't make it."

The Mercedes turned into the condominium parking lot. It had nearly been cleared of snow, but there were mountains of it on the periphery and in the corners, piled under the fir trees that skirted the condominium complex. J. D. stopped the car and looked over.

"Well, why don't you come over Christmas day? Gladys always prepares a wonderful feast and I know she'd want you to join us. Say 6 o'clock?"

Jennifer grasped her handbag and reached for the door latch. "No thanks, Mayor. I won't be celebrating Christmas this year."

The Mayor sighed. "It'll all work out, Jennifer. Things will look better after you've had some rest."

She stared with hollow eyes, as she opened the door and swung out. Before leaving, she turned back toward him. "Do you know a Mrs. Wintergreen, Mayor?"

The Mayor considered her question. "No, I don't believe so."

"Frances Wintergreen?"

"Doesn't ring a bell. Should I know her?"

"...No."

"Get some rest, Jennifer," the Mayor said.

Jennifer didn't look back at him. She closed the door and traipsed off to her apartment.

Inside, the silence was overwhelming. The walls seemed to close in on her. She felt dazed and defeated. There was no fire in her body. No life or hope. A sorrow came, so deep, that no diver would ever find the bottom, no grave digger would ever reach the coffin it was buried in. She covered her face with her hands, but she couldn't cry. Nothing would come. The bitterness was too thick, the anger too heavy, like a dark wet blanket. It was all she could do to collapse onto the couch and flop over on her side, lifting her feet, curling up like a baby. Minutes later, she fell into a deep sleep.

When she awoke, she glanced at her watch. It was almost 10 a.m. She sat up, rubbed her face and swept the room with her eyes. Stabbing memories began creeping back into her consciousness. She shot to her feet, looking about, as if searching for some kind of escape hatch, a way out, an escape route away from her thoughts, memories and responsibilities. She suddenly remembered something Mrs. Wintergreen had said to her at Harvey's Pond the night before.

"You're going to be tested," she had said.

What did she mean by that? Had she known that her shop would be destroyed? Without thinking, Jennifer heard herself call out. "Mrs. Wintergreen!"

It surprised her. The name echoed in the apartment. Then she recalled what Mrs. Wintergreen had said about Mrs. Stanton not accepting her help. Jennifer reached for her phone and called the hospital. She was connected to

Mrs. Stanton's room. Mrs. Stanton's niece spoke kindly to her.

"Mrs. Stanton has had x-rays and we're waiting for the results. She's still agitated, but she's been given a sedative. I'm sure she'll be all right."

Jennifer thanked her, offering apologies once again, then hung up. She turned in the direction of Harvey's Pond. She grabbed her coat and left the apartment, forgetting for a moment that she didn't have a car. She started off on foot toward the pond, pulling through the deep snow with urgency, feeling the sting of the wind across her face, feeling foolish, yet determined to find Mrs. Wintergreen.

About 20 minutes later, she arrived at the gazebo where she and Mrs. Wintergreen had talked. Someone had cleared the snow off the ice, and there were six people skating. One elderly couple, hand-in-hand, drifted easily across the pond, seemingly lost in the pure joy of each other, swaying gently in a perfect rhythm. It was as if nature were holding them up to her as an example of what she'd never have. She watched them for a time, jealously, darkly. The Christmas music from the speakers was Judy Garland singing *Have Yourself a Merry Little Christmas*.

Jennifer pushed her hands into her coat pockets, turned her gaze away from the couple and shaded her eyes from the now brilliant sun that was glaring off the ice. She didn't want to admit to herself that she was looking for Mrs. Wintergreen, and she felt pangs of anger for even being there. But she was desperate and had nowhere else to go. She had no one to talk to. She couldn't stay in her apartment and she certainly couldn't go back to town.

Like someone who was about to take a plunge into icy

water, she took a few deep breaths to fortify her courage, then started circling the pond. Half an hour later, she was hungry, her face was hard with cold, and she was bitterly discouraged. She turned slowly, searching all four directions, and then stared up into the blue dome of the sky. She stood on a hill overlooking the pond, hearing the soft rasp of an airplane passing over, glinting in the sunlight.

Then quietly, desperately, she whispered. "I'll go…"

At that moment, she spotted Mrs. Wintergreen below, skating beside the elderly couple. All three were laughing, gliding and performing a little dance. Jennifer jolted forward. She swiftly descended the hill, side-stepping, sliding, falling, bracing herself with her hands and hurrying over to the edge of the pond. She frantically waved, trying to get Mrs. Wintergreen's attention.

"Mrs. Wintergreen! Mrs. Wintergreen!!"

Mrs. Wintergreen did a skillful pirouette, whirling in circles like a top, finally coming to an abrupt stop. The couple applauded.

"Very good, Frances," the woman said.

"Nicely done," the man added.

"You gave me the lessons," she said, applauding them. "It only took me 30 years!"

Mrs. Wintergreen turned to Jennifer and waved. "Hi Jennifer. What a beautiful day!"

Jennifer waved again, shyly, nodding. "Yes…yes…"

Mrs. Wintergreen said her good-byes to the couple, turned and skated over to Jennifer. "Hello, my dear."

Jennifer let out a pent-up breath, suddenly agitated. "How did you know?"

Mrs. Wintergreen took off her sunglasses. "I heard about your shop, Jennifer. I'm sorry."

"Isn't that what you meant, when you said I was going

to be tested? How did you know!?" she asked, aggressively.

Mrs. Wintergreen ignored her. "Have you changed your mind? Didn't I just hear you say you'd go? That you're ready for the gift, the adventure?"

Jennifer twisted her hands, caught between irritation and desperation. She looked away for a moment, shut her eyes, and then opened them. "I don't know who you are… I don't know what's happening…"

"I don't have all the answers, either, Jennifer, despite what you might think. Do you accept my gift?"

Jennifer tilted her head to one side, avoiding Mrs. Wintergreen's eyes. She wanted to take a step back, but to where? She was afraid to hesitate and frightened to speak. There was a small part of her that believed Mrs. Wintergreen possessed some strange power, some extrasensory ability to fling her out into timeless oblivion, like a mad scientist shooting a home-made rocket into outer space toward an unknown destination. There was another part of her that was laughing wildly at the fact that she was even speaking to this crazy woman, who claimed to be some Christmas Spirit! How utterly and completely ridiculous!

"Well, Jennifer?" Mrs. Wintergreen said, staring patiently.

Jennifer winced, and then finally opened her mouth. "… All right…I accept your gift."

Mrs. Wintergreen smiled, warmly. "That's wonderful news, Jennifer."

"What do I do now?" Jennifer asked, fretfully.

"You'll find a ticket on your kitchen table for a flight to New York City that leaves at 2 o'clock today. Be on that plane!"

Jennifer's face fell apart. "Today!? New York! I've

never been to New York. I wouldn't know where to stay, where to go! I don't know anyone!"

"Don't worry. There are wonderful people in New York City, just as there are wonderful people in Oneida, Tennessee and here, in Willowbury. You have a reservation at The Plaza Hotel on Fifth Avenue. After that, the adventure will find you."

Jennifer was too stunned to speak. Mrs. Wintergreen took her hand and led her back to the gazebo.

"How long will I be there?" Jennifer asked.

"Time won't matter, Jennifer. Like I said, the adventure will find you and will give you everything you need."

Jennifer tensed up. "Will you be there? Will you be in New York if I need you?"

Mrs. Wintergreen held Jennifer's hand firmly between her red woolen mittens. Jennifer's cold hands immediately warmed. "You'll be fine. Understand something, Jennifer. This gift, this adventure, will require courage."

"Courage? What do you mean, courage? What's going to happen to me?"

"Nothing that you can't handle." She paused. "No more questions, now. Experience is always better than words. You'd better go or you'll miss that plane."

Jennifer hesitated.

"Go!" Mrs. Wintergreen said, gently pushing her toward the path that led toward the road.

Reluctantly, Jennifer started walking away, turning haltingly, throwing glances back over her shoulder at an encouraging Mrs. Wintergreen. When Jennifer crested the hill that led to the highway, she looked back again, and Mrs. Wintergreen was gone.

# CHAPTER 6

By the time the 727 taxied to the runway, Jennifer's named and unnamed struggles were replaced by a larger, and more immediate, anticipation and doubt. In her haste to pack, dress and call for a taxi to take her to the airport, she'd surely forgotten things—maybe a toothbrush or deodorant. She'd had no idea what to pack for New York—didn't have a clue what she should wear on "this adventure", and knew from experience that whatever she brought would be all wrong anyway.

In case she needed something more formal than the slacks she was wearing, she'd packed her burgundy dress and a green silk scarf. The dress was comfortable and it accented her figure; it had some sense of elegance she would undoubtedly need, if she was going to be staying at The Plaza Hotel on Fifth Avenue. Her garnet earrings, a gift from Lance, had fire in them, suggesting confidence. She'd need all the help she could get. She found some medium heels that matched the dress, but pinched her toes, especially her left ones, but she'd have to endure that discomfort for the sake of appearance. The boots she was wearing to travel in were warm and comfortable at least.

Just before she'd grabbed her suitcase and started for the door, she felt her hair falling all about her face, so she combed it straight back from her forehead and tied it in back with a blue elastic band. It made her crazy to have hair tickling her face when she was nervous. Maybe she'd lost her mind! Thrown away all logic and abandoned reason. She felt odd and disoriented, and she only hoped no one would ever find out what she was doing.

The seat next to her was empty, for which she was grateful. She was too restless to control her persistent squirming. She crossed her legs, and when her left knee began bouncing, she reached for a magazine in the seat pocket and thumbed through it absently.

Once airborne, she watched stringy clouds flee past the window like remnants of old dreams and memories. It seemed like time itself was racing by in a never-ending stream of forms, events and possibilities. As the plane rose higher, she stared into the endless blue sky, wishing she were as undefined and free. But too many questions intruded. "What would happen to her shop? Should she apply for another loan? Should she just leave Willowbury and move somewhere else? Why was she going to New York? What would happen?"

She took a deep breath, settled back into the seat and closed her eyes. Images flashed by. Her eyelids twitched, she grew heavy and was suddenly, utterly exhausted. She fell into a deep sleep.

When Jennifer awoke in startled surprise, the plane was gliding over Manhattan in a light snowfall. The view nearly took her breath: an endless vision of towers, glass canyons, bridges and water slid gently beneath her, like an exquisite apparition. She saw the veins of streets and highways; the Empire State Building and the Chrysler

Building, shiny and glorious. It was all a dream. A magnificent, special effect from some Hollywood blockbuster film. And she was in it! She felt the impulse to reach for the City, as it, somehow, seemed to be reaching out to her.

Lance had described New York to her many times during the weeks before they were to be married. He was anxiously anticipating playing tour guide on their honeymoon.

"New York's like a wonderland of the crazy, the playful and the hopeful," he'd said. "Whenever I walk the streets and look around, I believe that absolutely anything is possible—anything can happen… and many times it does."

Lance had been to New York three times: once on a high school band trip, once to a friend's wedding and, finally, to a medical conference when he was in medical school.

Jennifer's elation was suddenly smothered by the memory of a poem she'd found and read, repeatedly, soon after Lance's death.

*I weep, weep*
*for again the departure,*
*Your hand on the banister. Your glove on the stair.*

That's how she last saw him, on the stairs, his hand gripping the banister, looking down at her, lovingly. He'd simply said, "I'll see you tonight, honey."

That was it. "Honey" was his last word to her.

As she buckled her seatbelt in preparation for landing, she again felt a pain that she could not touch; a loss, unspeakable; a torment that deafened; a new and alarming realization that the taste of his warm lips was fading from her memory a little more every day. That brought a nagging guilt. How could she forget! How dare she! Lance would never have forgotten her! Never!

The pilot masterfully landed the plane, but as the wheels touched and screeched on the LaGuardia runway, she was jolted, not because of the landing: it was the recognition that she had arrived at the city of her unknown adventure. She could feel the proverbial butterflies trapped in her chest, fluttering; she breathed deeply to try to release them.

It was an easy taxi to the gate; the steady falling snow had produced little accumulation. When the seatbelt light went off and passengers stood, Jennifer noticed, for the first time, how light and happy everyone seemed—how ready for celebration—how the anticipation of Christmas hung in the air like the sweet smells of a bakery.

She slithered out between the seats and joined the line exiting the plane, feeling her shoulders slump forward, feeling the heat of uneasiness rise to her face. Would someone be waiting for her? Perhaps Mrs. Wintergreen?

But no one was waiting for her.

She followed the signs and the stream of passengers to the baggage claim area, and after she'd gathered her suitcase, she left the terminal, stepped outside into the cold and traveled toward the taxi stand. Sweat had broken out around her neck and on her forehead. She was not an easy traveler. Lance had teased her about it, not that they had ever traveled very far or often, but even short trips had made her nervous. There were just too many unknowns, things to forget, possible little disasters just waiting to happen. And something always did happen: a flat tire on their way to Florida to see his parents; a minor car accident on a rain-slicked highway as they traveled to Virginia Beach for a long weekend; and

Lance's dog, Oscar, charging off into the woods after a rabbit. It took Lance almost an hour to track him down in a freezing rain. He'd caught a cold and was in bed for two days.

Jennifer found the taxi stand and took her place in the long line. There was an almost frantic energy that she found unnerving and disconcerting. People stepped quickly, nudging and jostling her. Taxis bolted ahead, stopped abruptly, horns blared, people waved and shouted. The taxi dispatcher snapped his fingers aggressively, yelling at the taxi drivers and the impatient passengers. Some travelers hollered back at him, their faces firm, expressions challenging.

She joined the others, noticing some clutching their Christmas packages. Others snapped out cell phones and newspapers, waiting patiently, as if this kind of long line was as natural as waiting for the change of seasons. Children skipped and played, pointed toward the snow and dropped little candies into their mouths.

A few minutes later, Jennifer raised her chin to see that she was next. She glanced at the taxi dispatcher, a craggy-faced man with a gruff manner, and she shrank back. Her taxi arrived in aggressive fits and starts. It stopped, rocked—the trunk popped open. Jennifer hesitated, agitated. She wasn't sure she wanted to ride with this man! The taxi dispatcher's hands went to his hips in insulted impatience. He scrunched up his eyes into irritation, then flicked the bill of his captain's hat, puffed out his chest like a general, and threw an angry pointed finger at her.

"You! Go! Move!"

Jennifer snapped to attention, gripped her pull handle and stepped rapidly toward the taxi, hearing the suitcase wheels growl across the concrete. The taxi driver met her, a bearded man in a white turban; he lifted her suitcase as if it were a paperback book and tossed it into the trunk. She looked at it, distressed. She slid into the back seat to stifling heat, closed the door and peered nervously through the heavy Plexiglas window at the cab driver.

"Where to?" he called, in some strange accent.

Her heart was thumping in her throat. "The Plaza Hotel on Fifth Avenue. Do you know where that is?"

He barked a laugh, yanked the car into gear, and shot away. As soon as the taxi plunged into traffic, it seemed to Jennifer like a great battle of nerves, will and testosterone was in play. Cars darted from lane to lane, weaving, breaking, charging. Tail lights flashed; horns wailed in fear or warning or ego wounding, as a silver gray Buick Regal cut off a sleek red Porsche. In sudden defense, a forward taxi just managed a chaotic swerving maneuver to keep from slamming into both, but skidded into a bloated lane of buses and trucks, whose drivers welcomed him with clenched fists, angry cries and blasting air horns. A truck whipped into the left lane, brazenly, rupturing traffic and slinging water from its daring muscular wheels, in a remarkable display of oafish power.

The frenzied movement was disorienting and electrifying, like a kind of three-dimensional video game, with lasers, bells and whistles. Jennifer sat on the edge of her seat, eyes wide and alert, not recalling Lance ever describing a New York quite like this. They raced by monumental billboards that seemed to shout out their messages in bold letters and glossy images, to see the hottest Broadway shows and the newest hang-on-to-your-seat movies—or to stay at the savviest hotels.

Jennifer's cab driver seemed oblivious to it all, as he chanted, hoarsely, along with a CD in some mid-Eastern language, while fighting the cars and the road for survival and superiority.

When she saw the New York skyline looming in the distance, blazing against the heavy charcoal sky, her spirits lifted considerably. She'd seen pictures and movies, but nothing could compare to the stupendous live vision before her. It was magical. She felt a girlish excitement.

After they abruptly turned off the FDR Drive, she noticed shops, restaurants and office buildings, all decorated for Christmas: blinking white lights; extravagant wreaths with red ribbons; star bursts; and window displays. She was amazed by the sheer size of the city—the broad sidewalks and avenues, the buildings, close and towering. She could already feel a restless fervor as she looked out into the crowds of rushing people and the glare of lights.

When they approached The Plaza Hotel, Jennifer took in the 19-story structure and felt herself lift up. It looked like a castle out of a storybook; an opulent-looking French chateau! The taxi turned onto Central Park South, past horse-drawn carriages and Central Park, then turned left and rolled up to the entrance. She took in the glazed brick façade and saw doormen dressed in long red Edwardian coats standing by, as couples and families entered through the revolving doors with their designer shopping bags.

A doorman approached, tall and imposing, and opened her door, smiling. "Welcome to The Plaza Hotel!" he said, cheerfully.

Jennifer nodded meekly, then stepped out into a gentle snowfall that had begun to blanket the ground. Her cab driver reached into the trunk and tugged out her suitcase and handed it to the doorman. In a kind of hazy exhilaration, Jennifer paid the cab driver and turned toward the doorman, who led her up the red carpeted stairs, through the revolving doors into a resplendent marble lobby.

She saw expensive boutiques and shops, and crowds of lively children and well-dressed couples. She especially noticed the women. She thought they looked brittle and snobbish, even self-adoring, as they checked themselves out in the gilded framed mirrors and walked with calculated flair, as if a TV camera were following them. Even the young girls had a kind of stylized irritation, with their Bambi eyelashes and pouty mouths, as they ignored their parents, brothers and everyone else.

The men looked wan and milky. Thin, for sure, and elegantly dressed, but too self-assured and aloof for her taste.

Jennifer tried for a worldly, straight-backed dignity as she walked toward the front desk, but from the expressions of people who looked back at her as she passed, she was sure she had "Small Town Girl" written all over her face.

A middle-aged woman, dressed in gold and white and delineated with refinement, greeted her. "Good evening, my name is Eleanor," the woman said, pleasantly. "How can I help you?"

Jennifer said she had a reservation and quietly gave her name. A moment later, Eleanor nodded in agreement and began entering information into the computer.

"Yes, Ms. Taylor, you'll be in one of the Fairmont Deluxe rooms. That room has a king-sized bed and a city view. I think you'll be very comfortable."

Jennifer managed a modest smile. "Thank you, I'm sure I will be. Can you tell me who made this reservation, please?"

Eleanor nosed closer to the computer monitor. "Let's see… Yes…the reservation was made by a Frances Wintergreen."

Jennifer closed her eyes for a moment. When she opened them, Eleanor was looking at her, inquisitively.

"Is everything okay, Ms. Taylor?"

"Yes. It's just been a rather unusual day."

Eleanor finished processing the reservation, presented Jennifer with her room key and a glossy brochure filled with information about the restaurants, bars and boutiques. A friendly bellhop indicated toward the elevators, gripped the handle of her suitcase and led her toward them.

Once upstairs, the bellhop swiped her room card and stepped aside. Jennifer entered and froze. Her astonished eyes took in a spacious luxury of rose and gold. There were silk wall coverings, a sparkling antique crystal chandelier and a marble fireplace. There was an oak lounge table with matching chairs, a large oak writing desk with claw feet and a generous refreshment center. Jennifer stood motionless as the bellhop parked her bag by the bed and parted the rose-colored drapes. Beyond the towering windows, the city beckoned like shimmering jewelry.

She was still half-frozen when she tipped the bellhop. After he'd shut the door behind her, she stood, puzzled and transfixed, lost in a dozing daydream. She stood in the silence of anticipation, wondering what to do next. She turned toward the bed, a splendorous thing, and considered a nap. What if she slept through the night? Would her adventure come to her in dreams? Maybe from down the chimney of the non-working fireplace? Perhaps a spirit—a Christmas spirit—would appear and drag her off through the window and out over the city, similar to what had happened to Scrooge in Charles Dickens' *A Christmas Carol.*

She felt a chill. The cold inside tightened her. She ventured to the window and stared out, watching the lazy snowfall, hearing the murmur of city sounds: car horns, church bells, sirens.

She felt oddly displaced. The quiet seemed pregnant with mysterious personal potential. It was as if, with a little effort—perhaps a wave of her hand or a word uttered with the right emphasis and inflexion—she could break through that personal wall of silence and enter into a new wonder, like a child parting a scented bush to discover a secret emerald pond.

She drifted away from the window, back to the center of the room. She nervously dismissed the feeling as lightheadedness. She hadn't eaten since morning. She dialed room service and ordered a turkey club and coffee.

The temptation of the bed was too overpowering. She stretched out and closed her eyes, allowing her entire body to sink into the luscious quilted bedspread. After several deep breaths, she began to relax. There were no visions, no revelations. No adventure.

When the food arrived, she asked for the bill but was informed that everything was taken care of. She ate voraciously. A turkey club had never tasted so good and the coffee refreshed and warmed her. As she took the last swallow of coffee, she rose from the table, feeling a subtle nudge—an urgency.

"It's time to see New York," she said aloud.

She reached for her black woolen coat, red cap and leather gloves and left the room. Downstairs, she walked purposefully through the lobby toward the revolving doors, scarcely aware of her surroundings, the people or the sounds. That odd silence had returned, vital and throbbing. She shrugged it off, as she emerged from the hotel at twilight, to see the streets and sidewalks thick with people, the air alive with playfulness, as if a great treasure hunt was going on. She strolled by Bergdorf Goodman, Prada, Trump Tower and Tiffany & Company, passing sidewalk Santas ringing bells; hearing Christmas carols waft out of the stores onto the streets; watching the snow cover the streets, cars and people like a sugary icing.

Twenty minutes later, Jennifer crossed Fifth Avenue and started back toward her hotel, suddenly feeling a peculiar impulse to see F.A.O. Schwartz. As she approached, she saw him: a boy, no more than 6 years old, dressed in a navy down bubble jacket, red ski cap and forest green gloves. He weaved his way through the crowds, like an expert, like a little football player dodging tackles. There was a puckish energy about him, a bit of a swagger in his walk. To her surprise, he moved toward her.

When he was 20 feet away, he stopped and called out her name in a loud clear voice. Certain that he was calling for another Jennifer, she ignored him and progressed on, looking toward the little plaza in front of F.A.O. Schwartz, which was teeming with shoppers and tourists.

He called to her again. His voice was so loud and penetrating that she turned toward its source, searching diligently. She saw him standing firmly near the stairs, his hands in his pockets, staring at her with a kind of mysterious eagerness. She didn't quite know what to make of him. She was surprised at the sudden warmth she felt, and the strange familiarity in his face and eyes, as if he might have wandered in and out of her life either in the distant past or in a recently forgotten dream. She found him at once endearing, guarded and restless. As he stared, she became more aware of her loneliness—a loneliness so thoroughly embedded in her gut that she felt a throbbing, aching pain. A raw evening wind whipped her face. She grimaced.

Jennifer glanced about to see if this child was speaking to someone else, but no one else had responded. No one seemed to notice him or her. The bustling crowds pressed on, ignoring them. Jennifer studied this kid for a moment, calculating the distance between them. She started toward him.

He pivoted, descended the stairs, and hustled off north. Puzzled, Jennifer stopped. The boy whirled around and motioned, with his little gloved hand, for her to follow him. Reluctantly, she did, but with uncertain steps. Waves of people passed, bumped and jarred her. Falling snow blurred buildings and muffled city sounds. She edged around elbows, backs and shoulders and felt like a salmon swimming upstream, throwing darting glances ahead, to keep the boy in her vision.

She followed the boy across Fifth Avenue until they came to the edge of Central Park South. Then, just as she was gaining on him, the kid dashed away into the white snowy haze of the park, down a winding path and out of sight.

Jennifer stopped, bewildered. As she was catching her breath, that deep silence returned, as though someone were flipping switches, turning off the sound all around her. She turned in place, confused and frightened. Suddenly, she plunged into the center of that silence, as if falling through the thin ice of a frozen lake and sinking down into a black abyss.

Things began to slow down, like exhausted windup toys: people, cars, and horse-drawn carriages. Jennifer had the queer feeling that she, herself, was losing definition, was slightly out of focus—a nebulous sketch.

Twilight descended in a cool blue glow, back-lighting the flecks of snow and creating an eerie world of vague shadows and flickering images. The sky began to move; gray and burgundy clouds lowered and boiled through the Central Park trees, in a wind that came in cold punching bursts, scattering old newspapers, leaves and snow.

Jennifer stood mesmerized, staring helplessly. The ground began a slow rotation, scraping, rattling, as if she were on a revolving stage. Before her she saw a kind of open doorway, golden, shimmering and inviting. A gentle hand seemed to nudge her toward it. As she passed through, she witnessed a storm of images, like pieces of things in a wind storm, blowing, soaring and scattering. Time appeared to be rewinding itself, spinning wildly, as she looked out into a liquid world of fleeting visions of the 19th century. Buildings and structures appeared, and then crumbled into a dusty blue light. New ones shot up grand and tall, street scenes appeared like moving montages, and people went hurtling by like tumbling gymnasts, across an empty street. She heard church bells, muffled voices, sirens and the sounds of bombs and rifle fire. She was petrified and fascinated.

Then suddenly, everything stopped and fell into a deafening silence. Gradually, a new reality began to take shape: the sounds of clattering coaches; horses' galloping hooves and neighing; the blur of human voices; the vague, shadowy outlines of buildings and people. Her nose was assaulted by the sharp odor of horse droppings, and she sneezed.

Then suddenly, in front of her, a group of women approached. They wore lavish dresses and gripped dark umbrellas, staring at her strangely, indignantly, obviously spurning her. She was amazed at the clarity of detail: a long gown of royal-blue satin, an emerald gown trimmed with velvet and lace, a beautifully tailored gown of dark blue twill and cream-colored flannel. Their hats stood six inches high or more, with large brims and shallow crowns, made of burgundy or dark green felt, with dramatic plumes and feathers.

Her attention was pulled away to the street. A bright yellow carriage with shiny black fenders passed, followed by magnificently enameled coaches drawn by sleek black prancing horses and driven by proud liveried men with top hats and polished boots. She saw carriages of all sorts, a dray wagon, hired two-wheeled hackneys and horsecars all competing for the right-of-way, just as her taxi had done, traveling from the airport. Pedestrians seemed to bully their way through the intersections, taking their lives into their hands, some pausing to look back at her, with dark, curious eyes.

Men strolled the sidewalks, dressed in dark suits and boiler hats, smoking cigars. She could see the orange glow as they puffed and inhaled and blew the gray smoke skyward. They gave her the once-over inquiring glance, then moved on, shaking their heads. She stared in fright and wonder as riders on horseback looked back at her in surprise, regarding her as a spectacle and a kook.

Then, like a dissipating dream, the vision faded. Another world emerged. A world of beeping model-T Fords, bell-ringing trolley cars and clunky wagons carrying fat wooden barrels and bales of hay. Faces flashed before her in a kind of strobe light: hooded faces, bearded faces, faces with scars and pop-eyes, faces of the angelic and demonic, faces of children laughing, coughing, dying. Then, as if sucked away into some kind of cosmic vacuum cleaner, in an instant, all faces, buildings, cars and carriages disappeared into a ringing silence.

Everything stopped. Stopped dead! No movement or sound! An uneasy stillness pulsed.

Despite being anchored to the ground, Jennifer felt as though she were about to stumble, lose her balance and fall off the edge of the world. She grabbed a desperate breath, feeling the rise of a natural prayer for help.

Then she saw something. Something on the path where the kid had disappeared. She narrowed her frightened eyes. From deep in the park, on the winding path, a figure approached from a snowy fog—a figure covered by something—a sheer black cloth, like a shroud. The figure moved silently along the winding walkway, stiff-legged like an old man. Jennifer wanted to run, but she couldn't move. She wanted to cry out, but the sound caught in her throat. The figure moved toward her deliberately, the wind ruffling the edges of the cloth.

When the figure finally stopped, abruptly, and waited, Jennifer swallowed. She was cold, feeling as heavy as a boulder. A blast of wind swept in from the north and the shroud began to unravel. It whipped around the body in a circular motion, slinging the gossamer fabric wildly about in a maddening frenzy of flips and curls until it extended high above the figure, connected only to the neck. It fluttered like a dark sail, snapping like a whip in a forceful wind. Finally, it shot away and soared. Jennifer watched it rise into the burgundy-stained sky, over barren trees, like a dark kite, until it drifted out of sight.

Jennifer's eyes slid from the sky and lowered uncomfortably. She stared soberly, temples throbbing, as her eyes came to rest on the uncovered figure 25 feet away from her. It was Lance.

# CHAPTER 7

Jennifer was breathless from the sight of him. He wore a dark taupe parka, blue jeans and the oil-tanned waterproof boots he always wore in the winter. As he approached, his long brown hair scattered in the wind. He moved with an easy unhurried stride, as if he had made peace with time, as if patience had been captured and tucked away in his back pocket.

He stopped only a few steps away from her. Jennifer recognized the lively humor in his amber eyes, the fan of wrinkles around them, the soft lines in his still boyish face.

She stood rigid. She didn't believe what she saw. It was a tragic projection or an hallucination. She would simply stand frozen until it, or she, melted away. Until reality—her reality—returned.

And then Lance spoke in his light, airy tenor voice, as he took in the scenery. He grinned a little. "Well...I can't say I understand how these things work, but I think that someone must have gone a little overboard with taking you back in time. But then, it shows that life passes swiftly, and that our time on earth is brief. It's only been a year, hasn't it? Not a hundred."

Jennifer was silent. Her heart dared not take him in. She could easily shatter into pieces.

The sky became a quilt of white and gray. Falling snow softened the light. The wind played with the bare tree branches, rattling them as if to stir them from death.

"Let's take a walk, Jennifer," Lance said, reaching for her hand. "There's a beautiful spot not too far from here."

She clenched her teeth. Air escaped between them in sharp terrified gusts, puffing out white clouds of vapor, like steam from a train.

"Don't be afraid. It's all right. It's only me."

She shook her head, slowly, resolutely. She could not give in to the fantasy. "No! No... it is not you! I don't know who or what you are but you are not Lance. Lance is dead!"

Lance lifted an arm, searching for words. "Yes... in a manner of speaking, I suppose I am dead." He smiled warmly. "But I'm here now. And I'm real."

The sight of him was unbearable. Jennifer spun around and walked briskly away into a blaze of light and snow. She couldn't see or hear anything!

Lance called out and it echoed. "Don't leave, Jen! We don't have a lot of time."

She stopped. She shut her eyes.

"Please, Jen. Please come back. I have to talk to you."

Jennifer turned unsteadily. His expressions startled her. She knew all of them so well: compassion and expectation. They disarmed her. "Who are you?" she asked, with effort.

"You know who! It's me, Lance Russell."

She could only manage to force out, "How?"

Lance lifted his arms, then slowly dropped them back

to his side, letting them slap against him. "Come on, let's walk."

Jennifer felt an overwhelming rush of hope. She moved toward him, cautiously. His familiar smile cooled the heat of her confusion and fear.

The world gradually returned to reality, as if a great storm had nearly passed. Traffic noise droned; couples and families reappeared, rambling through the falling snow; children sledded on a hill nearby, screaming cheerfully. The world as Jennifer knew it was back, and it helped to calm her.

"Trust me, Jennifer?" Lance said, as he removed his glove and reached again for her hand. She wanted to touch him, to hold that hand, to feel the human warmth of him, but she was afraid.

He gently took her hand. She closed her eyes, savoring its warmth, trying not to think about his inevitable departure.

They started down a path into the park. Darkness settled around them. Park lights blinked on, casting a comfortable intimate light on the path of fresh, glittering snow.

"So, tell me, Jennifer," Lance said. "How have you been?"

Jennifer allowed her eyes to linger on him for a moment before she whispered. "I don't care about any of that right now."

"Well, I've heard rumors about you," he said, lightly.

"What rumors?" she asked, defensively.

"You know… cold stares, cold shoulders and a cold, cold heart."

"That's not funny."

"No, it isn't."

She let out a deep sigh. "God, I don't understand this, and I know that none of this is real, but I don't care. I'm beginning to feel alive again."

Lance turned, squeezing her arm. "Speaking of funny."

She raised her eyes. "What do you mean?"

"Well, you *are* alive."

"Only when I'm with you. When I'm not, I might as well be dead."

He grabbed her shoulders and looked directly into her eyes. "Don't say that! Ever!"

His sharp tone surprised her. "It's true."

He relaxed his grip and spoke tenderly. "You've got to forget me, Jen, and get on with your life."

She ignored him. "… How…did you get here?"

Lance narrowed his eyes. "I was given a gift—a kind of Christmas present, I guess you'd say, to come back and see you."

Jennifer turned away. "I'm sure I'll wake up in a minute and be relieved because I'll realize I'm not crazy." She faced him, trembling. "But I'll be completely devastated because you'll be gone."

"It's not a dream, Jen. I came because I had to. I couldn't stand to see you so unhappy."

"Oh, Lance," she cried. Her body grew limp as she leaned into his chest. "I knew that nothing—not even death—could keep us apart. I just knew it."

Lance's body stiffened as he searched for the right words. "Jennifer… you know I've always loved you."

"Of course, I know. You don't even have to say it. We both loved each other from the very beginning—from the first time we saw each other at my Christmas party, when we were 10 years old."

Suddenly, from above, a mother-of-pearl light descended toward them, floating like a bubble. It hovered over the ground in an open space, became a scintillating blue egg that cracked open and exploded, bathing the area with the fullness and beauty of a pastel dawn. Jennifer and Lance became like a still-life, detached, held by the glory.

Jennifer applied a gentle pressure to Lance's fingers. She smiled to herself because the whole scene was preposterous, a fantastic fiction being played out in three-dimensionality. But she didn't want to close her eyes, she didn't want to disbelieve. If she shut her eyes, the catastrophe of Lance's disappearance would be possible. She knew she was living in a fugitive moment, in some creation where destruction was imminent, but for now, she wouldn't try to understand. She would just make sure that she didn't release Lance's hand.

Low clouds began to churn and thicken. On the stage in front of them, a curtain of snow was parted by the invisible hand of the wind, and Lance and Jennifer saw images slowly appear and come to life, as if they were emerging from a thick fog.

There was a Christmas tree, full and radiant. The form of a living room took shape: a couch, a recliner, a television set, a roaring fireplace. About a dozen children, nine to eleven years old, were dressed in the colors of Christmas, sipping punch, munching cookies, laughing and talking. Two boys were dominating the room, contriving mischief.

A ginger-haired girl of 10 was standing near the fireplace, where one solitary stocking hung. The name JENNIFER was sewn into the red velour fabric in white thread. There was a shyness in her body language: downcast eyes and hands folded tightly behind her back; a worrisome look in her shiny eyes. She was watching one particular boy, a brown-haired kid with a lanky body and pugnacious face. Jennifer scrutinized the boy as he stealthily crept over to a living room plant, stole a final glance to make sure he wasn't being watched, and poured his cup of red punch into it.

Little Jennifer enjoyed the act and smiled. She gathered her courage and went over to him.

"Hi…" Jennifer said, startling him.

He whirled, caught in the obsession of his act. He leered at her. "What do you want!?"

She moved closer to him. "Do you like my party?" she asked, twisting her hands.

"It's all right."

"Do you like girls?"

He shrugged, suddenly uncomfortable. "They're okay."

"Do you think I'm pretty?"

His eyes wandered the room, evasively. "I don't know."

"Do you like me?"

He shrugged again. "I don't know!"

"But you've seen me around, haven't you? At school, I mean. I've seen you."

"Yeah, I've seen you around."

"Do you have a girlfriend?"

"No."

"I think you're cute," Jennifer said.

"So?"

"So, will you be my boyfriend?"

Young Lance was insulted. "No way!"

As he hurried away across the room, the front door flew open, too fast, too far. It slammed loudly against the back wall, with a loud BANG, alarming the children, who froze. Carefree expressions turned to terrified ones.

John Taylor entered, a big man standing wobbly and slack, like a child learning to walk. His face was red and swollen, hair recklessly askew. He groped for the door-knob, seized it in an over-exaggerated sweep of his arm and closed it, much too carefully.

The room was suddenly filled with quiet agitation—like a kind of evil had just stepped out from the shadows and was positioning itself for an attack.

Mr. Taylor measured the silent room's reaction to him, showing an intimate, guilty pain in his dazed, watery eyes. His ravaged face was gaunt with defeat and worry. Little eyes stared back wide and still.

Mr. Taylor's attention fell lazily on a slouching woman standing in a corner. She was prim and reticent, dressed in red, with a white satin trim around the high-collared neck. Her hairdo of blond twists and curls, obviously new, was a special treat for the party. It had been a pretty face once, a face now fallen into heaviness and cheerless resignation, since life had passed her by years ago. Mrs. Taylor tried to avoid looking into her husband's face, but lost the battle. She wilted even more when he examined her carefully, to read, again, their old novel of struggle, grief and disgust. But this time, he saw that the last page had just been rewritten. The ending was inexorably clear: her eyes were lusterless, blank, reflecting darkness. Not a flicker of love was left for him.

Finally, he focused his attention on his daughter, little Jennifer. All the eyes in the room followed his as his hesitant gaze came to rest on her. She stood shaking, in stabbing embarrassment and dread. Her father staggered. There was an absence of sound or breath in the room. It was a death for her. It was the final killing of a wounded innocence.

"I'm sorry, little princess," he said, reaching for the wall to steady himself. "I'm real sorry. You know you're my little princess. You'll always be my little princess..." Jennifer refused to look at him. He wiped his mouth and refocused. "Well... you all go on with your party, now. I'm real sorry."

Mature Jennifer watched her "little self" and remembered exactly what was going on behind the depths of her green eyes. The little girl was retreating to safety inside herself. She was leaving the hellish world of betrayal and fleeing heartbreak. Her family deformity had been made public: it was an unrecoverable humiliation and little Jennifer was certain she was to blame. She found a safe place inside her heart and hid there.

Little Jennifer found Lance's face near the Christmas tree. He smiled at her, a lopsided shy smile—a secret smile. She saw the Christmas tree lights dance in his boyish eyes. How she loved him.

The vision exploded like the snap of a flashbulb and Jennifer stumbled backwards, shading her damp eyes. She trembled and looked for Lance. He was there. "Let's get away from here."

# CHAPTER 8

The minutes that followed were painfully silent. Jennifer knew Lance was holding secrets, through his lowered eyes; his sudden frown of concentration; his unspoken words that seemed to hang in the damp air. There was no longer any need for her to believe that she was dreaming or that she had lost her mind. She was in the grip of something fantastic, and she knew no words for it, only the feeling of being dangled over a precipice by some unseen force she could only hope wasn't entirely malefic. Lance was the only reason she didn't break into a sprint and run for her hotel. Good or evil, it didn't matter what the outcome, as long as she could be with Lance, listen to his voice and feel the warmth of his body. That's all that mattered.

Snow fell through a silky black sky, drifting near the golden park lights, creating a moody intimacy and a bizarre sense of timelessness. Although there was a cold wind, Jennifer wasn't chilled; if fact, it was the warmest she'd felt in a long time.

With her arm intertwined with Lance's, she pulled him even closer. "I'm not going to let you go this time."

He seemed preoccupied and didn't respond. "Remember our senior year in high school?"

"Of course I do."

"That Christmas, just before school let out for vacation, the band played a concert at the mall."

Jennifer remembered it pleasantly. "It was so cold that night… and snowing."

"Remember my trumpet solo?"

"*The Christmas Song*! Of course. I could never forget it."

"I hope you forgot that I cracked on the high note. My lips were so cold…"

"Nobody noticed."

"Kathy Mason did."

Jennifer dropped her pleasant face. "Don't bring her up."

"She was a great pianist."

"I don't want to talk about her!"

The light around them became softly radiant. A frail beam fell upon the path before them and they stopped. The beam expanded out and around them, and a scene slowly materialized: the mall as it was that night ten years before. The 12-piece band members stood stiffly in the winter chill, dressed in various jackets, caps and boots, clutching their trumpets, trombones and clarinets. A tall conductor cued them and they began to play *The Christmas Song*, their instruments swaying gently, Christmas lights reflecting off the brass. Jennifer watched as Lance took a few steps forward, wiped his mouthpiece nervously and began playing his solo. A crowd formed near a 6-foot Christmas tree, and they gazed on, with dreamy expressions and swaying bodies.

Lance's face intensified as he approached the high note, his cheeks ballooned. Jennifer looked sideways and saw Kathy Mason standing alone, staring at him in glowing admiration. She was tall, sophisticated and pretty, with an elegant neck and expensive clothes. Her red lips were pursed as if she were kissing him, while he kissed the trumpet. Jennifer hated her.

She released Lance's arm, pulling her attention from the vision. "I don't want to see this!"

Lance spoke evenly. "You were jealous of Kathy, weren't you?"

"You know I was!"

"Why? Because she was from a respected family of doctors and lawyers? Or was it because Kathy's father loved her more than anything else? Or because the family was rich?"

"Because she was in love with you!"

"She encouraged me. She saw I had talent as a musician."

"Like she really knew."

"She became a concert pianist, Jennifer."

"And you're going to be a successful pediatrician. You're going to be respected and make good money. How much money do you think you can make as a trumpet player, Lance?"

With a start, Jennifer suddenly realized what she'd just said, as if no time had passed, as if Lance had never been killed.

She turned back to the drama before her, just as Lance cracked on his high note.

Jennifer looked pointedly at the Lance standing next to her. "See what I mean?"

Suddenly, the scene changed, as though someone had changed film reels. She and Lance were in high school, standing near a row of lockers. She was reaching into her locker to take out some books, obviously upset and brooding. She wore a bulky white sweater and brown skirt, light makeup, long hair, and bangs that hid her forehead. There was a wilted droopiness to her posture and facial expression, almost as if she were afraid to show her attractiveness.

Lance was dressed smartly in a burgundy sweater, crisp white shirt and navy blue trousers. Under his left arm were books, and he was leaning against the lockers, looking pensive and distant.

"Jennifer, all I'm saying is that we should maybe think about it."

"You just want to date her, don't you? You want to date Kathy Mason! Just come out and say it!"

"All I'm saying is that maybe it would be better for both of us if we dated other people for a while. We've been seeing each other for eight years."

Jennifer faced him, speaking forcefully. "No! Never!"

Kathy Mason approached from down the hallway. Her sexy walk suggested a bold belief in her powers of attraction. She ignored Jennifer and presented Lance a look of restless desire, backing it up with an alluring smile. As he struggled not to melt, it was conspicuously evident that Lance was her chosen darling.

"Hi, Lance. See you at band practice," Kathy said.

Jennifer eyed her darkly as she passed. "Little bitch!"

Lance quickly recovered. "Look, Jennifer, you need to get involved in some activity other than me. I mean, why don't you join the school newspaper or the choir... something. All you ever do is just go to class, study and hang around with me. This is our senior year. You should enjoy it."

Jennifer slammed her locker. "I hate this school. Everybody thinks they're so special—so superior!"

"No, Jennifer! That's how *you* think they are! Most of

the kids and teachers are okay, you know? You've just, like, closed off from everything and everybody."

Jennifer cradled her books in her left arm, looking at him crossly. "I don't need them—any of them! I don't need anybody, but you. I love you, Lance. You're all I've got, don't you see that! I'm never going to let you go, Lance. Never! If you ever leave me, I'll kill myself."

Lance grabbed her by the shoulders. "Don't say that! Don't ever say that!"

The scene slowly dissolved into another series of flickering images. Jennifer saw herself in the front hallway of her home, surrounded by suitcases.

Her mother was standing like a quiet shadow, her hands folded, head down. Mr. Taylor approached the two of them, then stopped abruptly when Jennifer passed him an impatient, caustic glance. He accepted her punishment, shoving his hands deep into his pockets and hunching his shoulders forward.

Mrs. Taylor spoke in a quiet, hesitant voice. "You'll call, won't you, honey?"

Jennifer carefully avoided her mother's eyes. "I doubt if I'll have much time. College is very demanding."

Mrs. Taylor nodded. "Well, we'll go visit you. It's only a couple of hours away."

Mr. Taylor spoke up. "Yes, I can drive your mother there. I'm a good driver; I like to drive."

Jennifer looked at him coldly. "Yes, dad, the police and most people in town know all about your drunken accidents."

He moved forward in mild protest and hurt feelings. "That was years ago, Jennifer."

"Two years ago, dad. It's a wonder you still have a driver's license."

"You can't forgive me, can you? You can't let go of it."

Jennifer didn't honor him with an answer. He finally turned and shambled away.

With a sinister, triumphant expression, she looked at her mother. "Like I said, Lance and I are going to be pretty busy. I'm sure you'll both have other things to do."

Mrs. Taylor began to shiver. "Please, Jennifer, don't shut us out of your life."

Jennifer looked at her with disdain. "You shut me out years ago when you stayed with that man!"

"That man is your father."

"No he isn't. He stopped being my father a long time ago. And I lost all respect for you for staying with him."

"Don't say that… Please Jennifer…" she pleaded, fighting tears.

"Why did you stay? He embarrassed us constantly. He ruined your life. My life! He couldn't hold a job, couldn't provide anything except humiliation. Why? Why didn't you leave him?!"

Mrs. Taylor straightened, defiant and proud. "Because he's my husband! Because he was sick and needed help. I don't have to defend his life or my life to anyone, especially not you! We did the best we could!"

"Forgive me, mother, but if that was your best, then God help you! Lance and I are going to make something of our lives. We're going to be successful and respected and have money and friends, and nothing's going to get in my way. When Lance and I finish college, we're going to come back to this town and show these snobs—all of them—just what success really is! Lance is going to be a pediatrician, and I'm going to get my MBA and eat this town alive! Then they'll stop looking at me like I'm some kind of freak to be ignored or pitied."

Mrs. Taylor's shoulders sank, as if drained of energy. When she spoke, her voice was barely audible. "Yes… Jennifer… I hope it will make you very happy."

Outside, a horn blew. Jennifer spun toward it, excited. "It's Lance!"

She grabbed her bags and fled the house, not turning back.

Outside, she scampered down the stairs and was met by Lance, who took her suitcases and swung them into the trunk. Jennifer got into the car and closed the door without looking back toward the house. After Lance closed the trunk and climbed in behind the wheel, he faced Jennifer.

"Aren't you going to wave goodbye to your parents?"

Jennifer stared ahead, coldly. "Why? I've waited for this moment for years. I waved goodbye to them a long time ago. Let's get out of here."

After Jennifer left, Mr. Taylor returned to the hallway where his wife stood, trembling, still staring out at the empty street through the parted doorway window curtains. Her eyes were wet with tears and filled with remorse. He gathered her into his arms and rocked her gently.

"She's gone…" Mrs. Taylor said.

"Yes… Give her time… she'll come back to us someday."

"No, John… I don't think so. I don't think I'll ever see her again."

"Where would I be without your love, Betty? Without your support and forgiveness? Where would I be?"

She looked at him lovingly and nestled her head into his shoulder.

As the images faded into the quiet snowfall, Jennifer slowly lowered her head, feeling a sickening regret. Lance wrapped a gentle arm around her shoulder and pulled her close. She refused to look at him.

"She died five months later," Jennifer said.

"I remember," Lance said.

"I didn't know she was sick."

"I know, Jen. I know."

"She was right. I never saw her again… If I had known…if she had told me, I would have gone to see her. I didn't know. I would have gone."

"Of course."

"I didn't remember being so harsh… I didn't remember that."

They started down a footpath between quiet trees and snow-covered benches, and then advanced toward an arching stone bridge that overlooked a frozen pond. They started across and paused about halfway. Jennifer ran her hand over the stone railing, raking off snow.

"I never forgave my father," Jennifer said, sorrowfully. "We said so little before he died."

"Yes…"

Jennifer wiped her moist eyes. "I didn't know what to say."

"What would you say now?"

"I don't know… Maybe I would have visited him more…Maybe I would have tried to find a conversation… I don't know."

"I saw him once before he died," Lance said.

She looked up, surprised. "You did?"

"Yes... He told me he loved you and was proud of you. Very proud of you."

"Did he?"

"Yes…"

Jennifer shook away the thought, turned away from his eyes and stared into the darkness. She forced a blithe tone. "What New York spots were you going to show me on our honeymoon?"

Lance looked skyward, ejected his tongue to feel the falling show. Jennifer giggled, remembering he used to do the same thing when he was a boy. He leaned on his left foot. "Rockefeller Center, Lincoln Center, Sachs Fifth Avenue, a few restaurants, a jazz club or two."

"Let's go!" Jennifer said, enthusiastically, tugging on his arm.

Lance looked out across the dark pond that suddenly began to brighten with the colors of sunset: rust, pink and blue. Jennifer turned toward it, apprehensively.

"No, Lance! No more! I can't bear it. Why are you doing this?"

"I have to leave soon, Jennifer."

She grabbed for him, frantic. "No!"

"I came to show you the truth."

"No…No!"

"It's why I came!"

"No! Let's get out of here! Let's run away."

"There's nowhere to run, Jennifer. Don't you see? You've been trying to run away but you can't. It's in you! You carry it with you!"

Jennifer heard a voice in the light and it sent chills up her spine. She turned toward it and saw Kathy Mason on the stage of an empty concert hall. She was older, in her late 20s.

She wore a gorgeous black dress, with a plunging neckline, two-inch heels and a shimmering choker of pearls. Her raven black hair fell sensuously upon her shoulders; her make-up and lipstick accentuated her full lips and dark eyes. She stood stiffly next to a glossy black concert grand piano, glancing frequently at her gold watch in nervous expectation. When footsteps approached, her attention was riveted toward them.

On the bridge, Jennifer pulled away and tried to run, but some invisible force stopped her, screwed her feet to the earth. Lance looked on helplessly, as Jennifer twisted and fought to free herself. Finally, resigned, she faced the light.

From out of the shadows, Lance appeared, taking Kathy eagerly into his arms and holding her in a passionate embrace. They kissed, long and fervently. Then Kathy pulled away, examining his face.

"Did you tell her?"

Lance avoided her eyes. "Not yet."

Kathy wrenched away, disappointed and frustrated. "When, Lance? This is ridiculous! It's Christmas Eve! You're supposed to get married tomorrow!"

"I know, I know!"

He began stalking back and forth. "Ever since I saw you at that concert two months ago, I've been trying to come up with the right words to tell her. I knew then that I was in love with you and that I had been in love with you ever since high school."

"And you're not in love with Jennifer?"

"Of course I love her, but like a friend. I mean, I care for her—we've known each other for 15 years, but she's just squeezed all the life out of our relationship. She's so frightened and emotionally demanding. I just can't live like that! I can't! I kept telling her over and over again that I didn't want to be a doctor, but she wouldn't listen. She had our lives all planned out and that's the way it had to be. She saw me as a pediatrician when we were 16 years old, and she wouldn't listen to anything else! Then, the next thing you know, I finish college and I'm going to medical school, because I want to make my parents and Jennifer happy. It wasn't until I saw you again that I realized how miserable I've been all these years!"

Lance returned to Kathy, looking deeply into her eyes. "I want to be a musician! I have always wanted to be a musician!"

Kathy stroked his cheek, lovingly. "You're a wonderful musician, Lance, and you will be a *great* musician! You can start your lessons again. I can introduce you to people. We'll be so happy, Lance. I know it! I just know it! We're perfect for each other…but you've got to tell Jennifer the truth. It's tonight or never. You can't put it off any longer."

Lance closed his eyes and sighed, massaging his forehead. "You don't understand the pressure I'm under. More than once Jennifer has said she'd kill herself if I ever left her."

"Don't fall for that! She was just manipulating you."

He opened his eyes. "I know. It's just that she's been a part of my life for so long; she's like family… But I have to tell her. I can't marry her! I love you!"

Kathy pulled him toward her and kissed him again, passionately. "I'll be waiting to hear from you. Tomorrow we'll have Christmas together. Now hurry! Go!"

"I'll be so glad when this is all over," Lance said.

The image dissolved and another appeared. Jennifer felt stabbing pains in her chest and stomach, a mounting dread. She was helpless and couldn't move.

Lance was driving along a deserted two-lane highway, in swirling snow, the frantic wipers sweeping the windshield. He wiped beads of sweat from his forehead, blinking, tensed at the wheel, dreading the unpleasant task before him. On the radio, *The Christmas Song* was playing, but he didn't hear it.

"I'm so sorry, Jennifer," he said, aloud. "I tried to be what you wanted me to be."

The car gathered speed as Lance was lost in a tangle of words and emotions, impatient to see Jennifer and conclude the whole business. He was taking the turns clumsily, driving erratically, foot heavy on the accelerator and too light on the brake. Snow blurred the road, the lights, the trees. Straining, his eyes sharpened on the ghostly neon lights of a roadside diner. He recognized it. He was only 15 minutes away!

How would Jennifer respond? Would she fly into a rage? Burst into tears? Why hadn't she seen the distance in his eyes during these last two months and realized he was pulling away from her? She'd refused to see the truth, even though he'd tried to tell her—tried to show her with his reticence, with his absences, with his silence.

But it was still his fault for waiting so long. He should have found the courage to tell her weeks ago.

As these thoughts washed over him, Lance began drifting over the center line.

He shook his head firmly, suddenly feeling overwhelmed with guilt. "It's not your fault, Jennifer. Please understand that I'll always be your friend—I'll always be there for you. It's just the old familiar story, damn it! I fell in love with someone else! I didn't want it to happen. It just did. I'm sorry! I am so sorry!"

As Lance took a sharp curve, he saw stabbing headlights charging him. There was no time to think. The urgent moment became dreamlike. Lance whipped the car left, but as he swerved, the back tires struck ice. They spun away into a hopeless chaos. Lance saw the oncoming headlights widening on him, like searchlights. He braced.

The cars collided in a cacophony of exploding glass, screaming tires and grinding metal. Lance's car was swept violently off the road. It slammed into a cluster of trees, its top crushed, tires spinning. The SUV dove into a ditch, bounced and stalled. The stunned driver tumbled out and staggered to the side of the road. Through falling snow, he stared in horror at Lance's battered, overturned car.

Central Park returned with a blast of cold wind.

Jennifer was devastated, blunted by the scenes that dissolved into falling shards of snow. She tried to cry, but could only manage a whisper, a strained kind of agonized wheeze.

Suddenly, the bridge began to vibrate, shift and slide away to the left, away from the park, rising into a white shimmering cloud of snow. Jennifer stood rigid, cold and lifeless. She shut her eyes so tightly that they hurt. She grappled with a sudden insanity.

When her eyes snapped open, she saw St. Patrick's Cathedral looming before her against the dark rusty sky. She blinked around. There were no Christmas decorations in any of the store windows that emerged before her. There were no cars, no people—not the hint of sound or movement. It was painfully quiet, as if she were the last person on earth.

A gentle rolling fog drifted ominously toward her. Her probing eyes observed it, seeking meaning or form. Suddenly, within its boiling center, a slender green stem appeared, curled, and ascended. A rosebud formed. It emerged, pulsing, swiftly reaching height and maturity. It burst open, like a new world, in layers of unraveling silky petals. Jennifer took it in, her face fixed in wonder, caught between dread and expectation. The petals surged out in perpetual waves of splendor and luster – a dynamic explosion of dazzling color, sweet scents, and low thunder that rattled the world. Overwhelmed, Jennifer turned aside, chest heaving. She squeezed her eyes shut, seeking escape.

And then it was over. There was silence; a silence that throbbed and lengthened and hurt.

Jennifer carefully opened her eyes. She swallowed hard. Before her, projected on a dazzling white cloud, she saw the image of a solid oak casket. Gradually, agonizingly, the clarity of form, size and recognition revealed she was standing inside a funeral home. She stood like a ghost, watching, observing Lance's casket. He lay within the lacey mother-of-pearl bed, peaceful and still, surrounded by floral arrangements of roses, lilies and irises.

Jennifer watched as if drugged, as figure after solemn figure passed, some weeping, others quietly withdrawn, lost in an unspeakable grief.

The front door opened and Kathy Mason appeared, dressed in black, eyes swollen from tears, face stricken with heartache. She started for the casket, dazed and weak, taking slow, measured steps. With a reluctant hand, she reached for the casket, but she failed. Her bleak and wan face fell into new anguish. She staggered, folded into herself and collapsed to the floor.

The entire image suddenly dissolved, and the fog dissipated in a circling cold wind. Jennifer was left alone in an aching darkness, feeling like she, too, were dying, as if her very skin were cracking and peeling away from her brittle bones.

Suddenly, a shaft of yellow light shot from the sky, and Lance appeared; as though a magician had mumbled an incantation, snapped his cape and stepped aside. Lance stood tall and motionless, eyes wide, posture stiff, like a manikin, only 30 feet away, on the steps of St. Patrick's Cathedral. Jennifer was in the deserted street below, her eyes measuring him.

Her heart did not leap at the sight of him, as it always had before. She did not feel beautiful in his sight; she did not hope or think of ways to please him, with words, stories, little gifts, a new recipe. Dreams of future Christmases, of hectic shopping, tree decorating and Christmas dinners faded, all faded. Christmas Eves spent before a roaring fire, with stockings hung; cookies baking; children sleeping, anxiously awaiting the morning, did not appear.

They would not grow old together, two little people seated on a park bench content with a life well-lived, remembering old stories, recalling how they'd first met and how it had changed their lives forever. None of it would happen. None of it would have ever happened. Lance had betrayed her.

Inside she felt the eruption of an earthquake. A sudden and terrible violence swept over her: falling towers, great fires and deep angry chasms, swallowing up old hopes, beliefs and dreams. Jennifer watched them all shrivel up in the heat of destruction, being consumed by the furious fire, leaving nothing behind but dark, ravaged and barren land.

Lance waved. "Goodbye, Jennifer. Goodbye. I'll always love you."

He climbed the stairs and looked back at her once more before disappearing through the doors of St. Patrick's Cathedral. As she stood there in that miraculous silence, her old life ended in tremors of anguish and grief. She wept as she had never wept before, her shoulders rolling, her body shivering, in the muted light.

# CHAPTER 9

Jennifer heard the ringing of a bell in the silence of the cold night. There wasn't the slightest hint of life anywhere on Fifth Avenue: no people, cars or lights, and certainly no signs of Christmas. The streets were dark and ominous, disturbing to view, leading only into tunnels of alarming shadowy bleakness, where all life ended. The buildings were windowless and faceless, dusky with indefinite shapes. It was as if a dark catastrophic cloud had descended, covered the sun and snuffed out the light of any life—except for the single blue spotlight that illuminated St. Patrick's Cathedral. A sudden and sharp wind swept in and blew the red cap from Jennifer's head. It skipped and bounced away into the darkness, like a flat stone across a lake.

Jennifer was disoriented, sick and lost. As she looked about, fear seized her by the throat and seemed to pull her toward dark tunnels of despair and death.

But then she heard it. The ringing of a single bell. A single bell ringing caught Jennifer's attention. It wasn't loud or close, or coming from the church. It had an intimacy about it, like the nocturnal cry of a night bird for its mate, with its steady ring-da-ding-ta-ding, ring-da-ding-ta-ding, persisting, and hopeful.

Jennifer slowly lifted her heavy head and adjusted her stiff and punished body to face the direction of the sound. That's when she saw him again: the little boy she'd seen earlier, who'd led her to Lance. He stood a short distance away, dressed as before and looking at her with the warm, friendly, brown eyes of a puppy.

Suddenly, Fifth Avenue exploded to life all around her. Lights flashed on. Buildings shot skyward and windows glowed, shoppers hustled, cars advanced and honked; a sea of colored lights blinked on, in waves, rolling and leaping from window-to-window, street-to-street, like joy itself, until the entire area was ablaze.

The little boy motioned with his green mittens for Jennifer to follow him, and she did, wooden-like, through the steady crowds across Fifth Avenue and down West 50th Street toward Rockefeller Plaza, while the bell continued to call, not as a warning, but as a welcoming.

As they turned left into the Plaza, she saw it: the majestic Rockefeller Center Christmas tree, tall and glorious. Waves of crowds stared in wonder and joy. Lovers embraced, families roamed, ice skaters glided by below and shoppers toted bags, snapping photos with phones and cameras. Jennifer felt nothing. Her heart was cold. She stared dispiritedly.

Still the bell rang out, much louder now.

Jennifer spotted the boy again. He had found a short, portly Santa Claus, who stood off from the main thoroughfare. His bell was the source of the ringing. He swung it in an easy arch, his smile engaging and warm. The bell had the comforting, euphoric sound of distant church bells on Christmas morning, but Jennifer stared at the Santa, too preoccupied to notice or care.

He was dressed in the traditional red Santa suit, but the cloth seemed richer, finer, and more authentic somehow. His red cap was cocked coolly to the right of his burly head, and his white beard flowed in generous curls that reminded Jennifer of little meringues that topped desserts. The black, white-laced belt was broad, circling a generous stomach; the boots a shiny black, like the color and texture of the finest licorice. He stood next to a 3½-foot paper Mache chimney that held money, collected for the needy. People passed and dropped in coins and bills.

Jennifer approached him carefully, scrutinizing his jovial ruddy face.

"Merry Christmas, Jennifer," he said, softly.

Their eyes met. His dark eyes were lustrous and calm, like quiet pools. She was drawn there, into their wisdom and strength. It was as if he'd seen the entire spectrum of human existence, in all its beauty, folly and madness, and had participated in it all, joyfully, embracing it all with enthusiasm, compassion and humor. There was no judgment in his expression, no weakness in his stance. On the contrary, he stood strongly, as if he possessed the courage of a lion.

"Merry Christmas, Jennifer!" he said again, brightly.

Jennifer couldn't bear the radiant joy in his face. Not now. She shaded her eyes and looked away. All she could manage to say was, "Yes…"

He continued ringing the bell, saying nothing, occasionally glancing her way with the glittering eyes of a jokester. When he did, she felt a startling warmth well up from inside her chest. A moment later, she lifted her hand to her chest, and Santa noticed.

He presented his face toward the sky. "It's a beautiful snowfall. After all these years, it still makes me happy to see a beautiful snowfall. Don't you agree, Jennifer?"

Jennifer stared with glassy eyes, still feeling wounded and vulnerable. "I suppose so."

"It's my favorite time of year, you know," Santa said.

Jennifer didn't try to hide her irritation. She glared.

"You've had a difficult experience. It takes time to work through those things. I'm going to help you."

"I don't need help. I want to be alone!" Jennifer shot back, hearing the cutting tone of her words.

"Yes, sometimes that's good. But you've been alone too long..." He paused. "Have you finished your Christmas shopping?"

Jennifer took a breath. "Aren't you supposed to take care of that? I mean you are Santa Claus, aren't you?" she asked, sarcastically.

He grinned, broadly, with sudden surprise. "Well, yes, I suppose I am."

"What do you mean, suppose you are?"

"Well, let's just say that I'm the Spirit of Santa."

Jennifer sighed heavily. She looked away in irritation.

He chuckled. "Look around, Jennifer. Look into the faces of all these people. Take a good look, a generous look. A courageous look! Look how beautiful they all are! Look at the families: the fathers, the mothers, the wonderful children! Watch as the parents point their children's eyes to the lights, to the ice skating rink, to the glorious decorations. Watch as they listen to the church bells, to the Christmas carols, to the children's laughter. It's Christmas, Jennifer! Magical and spectacular Christmas!"

Jennifer looked at him with tired eyes. "I've seen it," she said, flatly.

Santa regarded her with surprise. "Really? Have you really seen it—heard it—truly experienced it in your heart, Jennifer?"

"Yes!"

"Well, after your recent shock, perhaps it needs to be reheated a little, like a cold cup of hot chocolate."

A man in a tattered coat approached the chimney wearily. He dug down deep into his pocket and extracted a quarter. He dropped it into the chimney, and then shambled off.

"Did you hear him?" Santa asked.

Jennifer shook her head. "Hear what? I didn't hear anything."

"He said, 'Thank you.'"

"Thank you? For what? He looked like somebody should be giving him money. He looked like he might even be hungry."

"He *is* hungry."

"So what's he so thankful about?"

Santa shrugged. "His secret, I guess."

Santa indicated toward the crowds. "All of *them* are spirits of Christmas, Jennifer. They create it. Without them, none of this would be here—I wouldn't be here. Without joy and honest celebration, without love, we would be living in that bleak shadowy darkness you just came from. No light… no companionship."

Jennifer trembled and whispered. "I'd like to go home now."

"And you will, Jennifer," Santa said. "You will go home."

Jennifer looked away in sad impatience, folding her arms tightly. "What's the point of all this?"

Santa didn't hesitate. "Your happiness."

"My happiness!?" Jennifer exclaimed, incredulous. She motioned toward the crowds. "Look at all these people. Are they happy? Why not help them? Why am I so special that I've been chosen to have happiness?"

"Why are you so special that you shouldn't have been chosen to have happiness?" Santa said, chuckling again.

Jennifer looked at him, pensively.

Santa stepped closer to her, swinging the bell, enthusiastically, the sound filling the plaza. "In this world, Jennifer, one person's happiness is so important because it can make such a big difference. It becomes contagious and touches many others, like a happy potion that is passed from one person to the next and cures many aches and pains. Happiness and love change the world from hell into paradise."

Jennifer shook her head. "Happiness and love don't last. Nothing lasts!"

"They last, Jennifer. They're the only things that really do last, but you have to discover them—work at them. They are wonderful journeys—the best adventures—but they take the greatest amount of persistence and courage."

Jennifer's eyes clouded up with angry tears. "My happiness, my love, was Lance! Until now, at least I had the memories of him—the memory that he loved me. That got me through the days and nights. What do I have now? Nothing!"

"Is that all you want out of life, Jennifer, to just get through the days and nights?"

She gave him a harsh stare. "I've lost everything: my business, my dreams, and the person I loved more than my own life, my own breath! So, if you want to make me happy, just stop doing whatever it is that you're doing, and leave me alone!"

Santa continued ringing the bell, and as he did so, Jennifer continued to feel warmth in her chest. She pointed toward the bell. "What is that sound? That bell? I've never heard a bell like that before."

"It's the sound of peace and freedom," Santa said.

"Peace on Earth, goodwill toward men?" she asked, cynically.

Santa smiled. "… Goodwill toward men, women, children and all things, yes."

"You're a dreamer," she said, dismissing him.

He rang the bell louder and laughed. "Yes, Jennifer, I am. I most certainly am!"

Jennifer searched for the child that had led her to Santa. "Speaking of children, where's the kid who's been leading me around?"

"He's lost."

"Lost. He's so small. Can you help him?" Jennifer asked, concerned.

"Perhaps when he comes back, we both can," Santa said, taking off his hat. "Speaking of 'back', I'm wondering if you'll do me a favor. I have a little errand to run, but I can't leave the chimney filled with money, and if I take the chimney with me, people won't have the opportunity to give. Would you please put on my hat and ring my bell while I'm gone?"

Jennifer pulled away, throwing up her hand in resistance. "No…I'm sorry, but, I… No, no way. "

"Please, Jennifer, I'll only be gone for a very short time."

Jennifer looked about, anxiously. A steady stream of people approached, dropping money into the chimney and nodding happily at Santa Claus.

"This money helps the people who need it, Jennifer. It will help the man you saw earlier. Please?"

Jennifer made a sour face then reluctantly snatched the hat from his hand. She shook her head at her own folly, waited, and then finally slapped the cap on. Santa handed her the bell. Grudgingly, she took it.

Santa laughed generously, a deep and hearty laugh that Jennifer felt reverberate throughout her entire body. It almost cheered her, but she was in no mood to be cheered.

"Don't be gone long," Jennifer said, already regretting her decision.

"I'll be back before you know it, Jennifer."

Jennifer stood by the chimney in a self-conscious posture. She gripped the warm wooden bell handle and then, quite surprisingly, felt the rush of something fantastic pass through her body, like a delightful electric current that quickened her pulse with a new vitality, lifting her spirits and her posture. She stared down at the heavy bell in suspicious bewilderment. As she lifted the bell to begin swinging it, she was surprised by the comfortable weight of it, by its luxurious golden luster, which she hadn't noticed before.

Slowly, with clumsy effort, she lifted the bell and began to swing it. At first, the iron clapper gave off a hollow metallic sound. Jennifer adjusted her stance and tightened her grip on the handle. She tried again. Gradually, she found a comfortable swinging rhythm and she threw her arm into it. It rang out clearly. People began to notice and smile.

As the crowds passed, she viewed them shyly, certain that they would look upon her as an intruder, as a curiosity, but they didn't. They smiled warmly, placed money into the chimney, greeted her with "Merry Christmas" and thanked *her* for the act of generosity.

Then, a remarkable thing happened. As people approached the chimney, she became aware that she could actually hear their thoughts! Their voices were as clear as if they were speaking to her!

A well-dressed man came by and dropped in a five-dollar bill. "I hope this helps end homelessness," she heard him think. "Well, at least it's something," he concluded. He nodded to her, affably, and walked away.

A young woman came over, dressed in a thin nylon coat, holding the hand of a little girl of perhaps 7 years old. The girl's eyes reflected the magic around her. The woman opened her purse, took out a dollar and carefully placed it in the chimney. She paused and closed her eyes, as if in prayer. "Dear God, thank you for the apartment… please, I just need $200.00 to get me through the month… I know you can help me. I hope this dollar helps someone."

The little girl looked up at Jennifer. "I love the snow. Do you love the snow?"

Jennifer nodded, uncertainly. "It's…okay, I guess."

"You don't look like you love the snow," the little girl added.

Jennifer narrowed her eyes. "I do, okay? I like the snow!"

The woman opened her eyes, smiled timidly, took her daughter's hand and started off. The little girl turned and waved at Jennifer, smiling happily, as they disappeared into the crowd. Jennifer returned a strained smile.

A muscular, stiff-haired teenage boy wandered over, looking about sheepishly, as if hiding from friends. He kept his eyes focused on the ground as he approached the chimney, pulled a wad of singles from his pocket and quickly tossed them in. "Please help my dad find a job."

He hurried away.

A moment later, a man walked over, opened his wallet and dropped in $20. "What a great city. I love this town.

Hope this money helps somebody."

A couple with two children came by. The woman dropped in $10. "Dear, dear Charlie… I hope you're happy in heaven. We think of you every day. How I miss you, my little one. This $10 is for a little child who may need some food or a safe place to sleep. I'm giving it in your memory."

A child hurried over and dropped in a quarter. "I hope Santa brings me a new brother."

Jennifer began to hear a multitude of thoughts, converging in upon her from all directions.

"Please bless others with this offering and help me with my arthritis. My knees are so sore."

"I can't wait for our baby to be born so we can show him Christmas!"

"I'm getting so old; I can barely see the tree. Here's money for young ones to see the tree after I'm gone."

"I miss my mother, she loved Christmas so much."

"I'm so lonely; this is such a lonely time of year for me. I wish I could talk to someone."

"I wonder if my boyfriend's going to get me that leather coat."

"I hope she's not expecting me to buy her that coat. No way I make that kind of money."

"That fake lady Santa Claus looks really sour. Who wants to see a face like that at Christmas?!"

The last thought shocked her. She threw darting glances about, to see if she could find the source of it, finally spotting the same boy who had been leading her around. He stared at her intently, as if working on a thought, but not disclosing it. Jennifer tilted her head toward him, like a robin listening for a worm, hoping to pick up additional thoughts. She waved at him, but he spun around and ran off into the crowd.

Santa returned and Jennifer sighed in relief. "Am I glad to see you," she said, pulling off the hat and handing it, and the bell, back to Santa.

He took them happily, returned the hat to his head and presently began ringing the bell. Jennifer became aware that she could no longer hear thoughts. Her shoulders relaxed.

"Did you enjoy yourself?" he asked.

"Enjoy? How do you stand it?"

"Stand what?"

"Hearing all their thoughts. It would drive me crazy."

"It was a gift to you. You heard the voices of their hearts: what they truly felt, needed and wanted. Were you moved by them?"

Jennifer massaged her eyes, weary and confused. "Yes…of course, but, what can I do about them—any of them? What can anybody really do?"

"Small things, Jennifer. Sometimes it's just a smile, a good wish, a generous ear, or even just the simple understanding that we're all here together on the Earth. That can lighten the heart."

He continued. "At Christmas, many people are thankful and happy, but there are many who aren't; their hopes, needs and fears are often more sharply felt, so we try to help them now and throughout the new year.

"By your just standing here and ringing the bell, you provided people with an opportunity to give, share and express what's in their hearts. I think you'll agree that most of the hearts in the world are good. And everyone wants happiness, don't you think?"

"Sure…I suppose."

"You just gave them a wonderful gift, and you asked for nothing in return. That shows generosity, Jennifer, and a good heart."

Jennifer noticed there were nearly four inches of snow on the ground. The wind was gentle, and traveling on it was the scent of pine and mint. She lifted her nose as the breeze washed across her face like a cool liquid. She looked toward the towering tree and the bustling crowd, lost in thoughts of many dimensions. Her mind struggled to find something to believe in, to hold on to. What astounded her was that she could still feel the dull ache of Lance's parting, but it had subsided dramatically, thanks to the warmth from the ringing bell; and that warmth continued to spread throughout her body like a healing balm.

He came from around the tree, his hands in his pockets, looking at her expectantly. It was the same little boy as before. Jennifer straightened and glanced over to Santa. "There he is again!"

"He needs your help, Jennifer. Follow him," Santa said.

"My help!? He keeps running away."

" 'A little child shall lead them'. Follow him, Jennifer; he'll lead you into your future."

Jennifer looked at the boy, who was again motioning for her to follow him. When she turned back to Santa, she froze. He was gone! Another Santa, taller and skinnier, was standing there, ringing a very different bell, a bell with a completely different sound: high-pitched and shrill. Jennifer wiped her eyes and tried to understand.

She turned her attention again to the boy, who kept waving her on. She followed.

# CHAPTER 10

Jennifer pulled her way through crowds, traffic and the blur of lights as she followed the child down snow-filled sidewalks to Lincoln Center. There, a large crowd gathered under another magnificent Christmas tree in the center of the plaza surrounded by the Metropolitan Opera House, the David Koch Theatre and Alice Tully Hall. As the crowd sang, inspiring voices and a brass quintet filled the air with "*Deck the halls with boughs of holly, fa-la-la-la-la, la-la-la-la.*"

Jennifer was looking everywhere for the boy, who, once again, had slipped away into the crowds and disappeared. The music was so delightful and captivating that she stopped and listened, viewing the animated, happy faces and the dancing children.

She heard a trumpet! Instantly, she stood on tiptoes to find the player. The tone was warm and joyful; the musician was an obvious master. She found him on the stage above the crowds, dressed in a red and green muffler and bright red cap. He looked nothing like Lance; he was heavier and older. But he played effortlessly, swinging to the playful rhythm, his eyes alive and glowing with happiness. Though he didn't look like Lance, she thought of him, felt again the pain of loss, then a tug of remorse. Why hadn't she listened to Lance when he'd told her how much he loved music, when he explained how alive he felt whenever he remembered his high school days and the solos he'd played? How excited he was whenever he played even a few notes for her? She'd often ignored him, passing it off as frivolous, a waste of time. Sometimes, she'd even walked out of the room in the middle of a phrase.

Her own voice echoed back to her.

"Grow up, Lance! You can't make any money at it! No one in town is going to respect us if all you do is play the trumpet!"

"Is impressing people in town so important to you, Jen?" he'd once asked.

"Your family was always well-off. I've been poor and pitied my whole life! I'm not going to let you give up being a doctor, a profession that pays well and is respected, to become a trumpet player, so we can be poor for the rest of our lives!"

Jennifer slowly dropped her head to her chest. The trumpeter began to play a solo: *The Christmas Song*. People near her sang along quietly: "*Chestnuts roasting on an open fire…*" It was so liltingly poignant that it brought tears, tears of regret, tears of appreciation. She wiped them away as she scanned the quiet, enraptured faces watching the soloist; faces filled with contentment and happiness. The music had taken them into another world, into another state far from the realities of life, where words and concepts simply dissolved. She felt her own heart become tender, and, to her surprise, she noticed that her shoulders and neck had relaxed, her body had settled more easily into the Earth; into the Earth that was bearing the weight of all of them, of all things.

"How is it that I've never felt this connection before?" she thought.

She could feel the music penetrating through the crust around her heart.

"I'm sorry, Lance. I'm so sorry," she whispered.

After the song was finished, the little boy appeared again, and then shot off toward Broadway. Jennifer called out after him, but he didn't stop. She wanted to stay, she wanted to savor the new feelings she was discovering, but she knew she had to follow the boy, so she slowly turned away and started after him.

It seemed like only minutes had passed when she arrived at a toy store, a tall bright red building, with yellow flashing lights and windows that danced with color, movement and animation. She watched as the little boy ran inside, underneath the arms of grown-ups toting large packages and bulging shopping bags.

She went after him. Inside, children darted about the shop with big, bold eyes and anxious bodies, exploring, squealing and pointing. Five-feet-tall stuffed animals loomed in the corners and on the stairways, miniature monkeys clung to railings, electric trains tooted and circled. There were racks stuffed with board games, dolls, brightly colored plastic trucks and walking robots. Parents struggled to contain the young ones, salespeople hurried by, and cash registers rang loudly.

Jennifer searched for the child, stepping past pastel-colored dollhouses, miniature forts and Victorian homes where puppets' heads were peeking out of windows.

She finally spotted him looking down at her longingly, from the second floor balcony. She started after him. Upstairs, she circled the floor, twice, pushing through persistent crowds, but not finding him. Finally, she stopped, mystified. That's when she overheard the conversation between two women, the next aisle over.

She ventured a quick look but could see only the back of one woman, dressed richly, in a fur, and the other, dressed modestly. They were strolling aimlessly through the aisle, and had paused to squeeze a cuddly little stuffed kangaroo.

The woman in fur said, "Don't waste your time unless this boy has money, and a lot of money. I don't care how nice he is."

"But he loves what he does," the other said.

"There's nothing worse than a man who loves what he does but makes very little money doing it. It's outrage posing as sanctity!"

"You were in love once."

"Once was enough."

"Don't you miss being in love?"

"I have his memory and my money. That's enough for me. To hell with the rest of it."

"But, don't you get lonely?"

"Look, Emily, it's time you started living in the real world, and the real world is a place where money and power are more important than love and romance. Love is a cheap sparkler. Love is fickle. Love dies. Believe me, you can get a little romance whenever you want it, if you have money. If I get lonely, I can always find a man."

"But what about children? Didn't you ever want children?"

"There are plenty of those running around already. Just look! Everywhere! You can barely walk the streets or the stores, for tripping over them. Don't be fooled into thinking that having children is so wonderful. If you look into the faces of most of the parents in this store you'll see nothing but stress, exhaustion and regret. When they grow up, they're even more trouble, and they cost a fortune!"

"Surely you don't believe that, Ms. Taylor?"

"I do indeed! And now I'm sorry I agreed to come with you to buy this silly gift for your little brother. I hate these stores, and their prices are so offensive!"

"You know, Ms. Taylor, my family wonders why I stay with you."

"We both know it's for my money, Emily. You think you'll get some someday if you're nice to me. Well, you're only a fair secretary, so I wouldn't push it."

Jennifer felt her way along the aisle until she was able to steal a look around the corner and catch a glimpse of them. When she saw the woman in fur, she stood bolt erect, her heart kicking in her chest. She recognized the woman immediately! It was herself! Older, yes, but she knew in her gut that she was looking into her own face: a sour face of a shriveled woman, old before her time, with cold hawk-like eyes and a shuffling gait, as if even her steps were stingy and resentful. She exuded a poverty of spirit that depressed the very atmosphere around her.

After they had drifted away downstairs, Jennifer leaned back against the pink wall, panicked. She watched the hanging cherubs and spinning angels above, looking back at her with daring eyes, critical eyes, beady eyes that warned and threatened. Sweat popped out on her forehead. Her heart raced. She wanted to scream out and run away—find someplace to hide—some sanctuary. After a deep breath, she spiraled down the wrought iron stairs and burned past shoppers, hitting the front door with the flat of her hand.

Outside, it was still snowing, driven by a stiff breeze.

She looked up and down the street, but nothing was familiar and nothing felt safe. She didn't know where to go.

When the child appeared, waving for her to follow him, she hesitated, fearing another painful encounter.

She shouted at him. "Who are you!? Tell me! Who are you!?"

He didn't speak. He just stood there, looking at her with pleading eyes.

"I'm not going anywhere until you tell me who you are!"

The little boy turned around and started off into the moving shadows. Lost and anxious, Jennifer went after him.

She followed him across Central Park West, and entered Central Park near 72nd Street, where all traffic had ceased and all things seemed to be in a state of uncertainty. The child hurried along the meandering pathway, and she struggled to keep up, stepping gingerly, watching him steadily as he forged ahead. When he crested the top of a hill, he stopped for a moment and looked back to her, and in the muted glow of the park lights, she saw snow falling about him.

"Wait!" Jennifer called.

To her surprise, he did.

She was nearly out of breath when she drew close to him. He stood motionless as she looked him over, trying to understand.

"You'll meet him soon," the little boy said.

"Meet who soon?"

"You'll see."

"Tell me. Who will I be meeting?"

He finally spoke. "Will you go sledding with me?"

"Sledding?" Jennifer repeated, confused and shuddering.

He nodded, then pointed toward the next hill, where Jennifer saw children swarming the slope, shouting gleefully. She squinted to see them streaming down the hillside on sleds and red saucers. She watched them building snowmen and having snowball fights.

Before she could answer, the little boy tore off toward the sledding hill, tumbling and sliding. She watched him climb and crawl until he crested it, triumphant and waving.

The wind scattered Jennifer's hair and she raked it from her face, feeling the damp snow. Her feet were cold. Her ears were cold. Her face was cold, and she would have given anything to be sitting by a warm fire with a hot cup of coffee. But she looked about, resigned, then started down the bluff, toward the boy. With great difficulty, she tramped down one hill and scaled the side of another, finally clawing her way to the top, tired, chest heaving.

She stood, slapped the snow from her coat, and stared in wonder at the delightful chaos of children rushing, shouting and romping in the snow. Parents pulled up the collars of coats, held back the barking dogs and poured and passed around hot chocolate from thermoses. The sight of it comforted her and gave her a sense of peace. She folded her arms to warm herself while she watched.

Moments later, Jennifer saw her little guide coming toward her, tugging a 60" Flexible Flier Sled—made of solid oak—one she hadn't seen since she was a girl! She stepped toward it and leaned over to examine the multiple ribs and steel runners.

Her eyes lit up. "It's beautiful. I used to have one of these!"

His face was alive and eager. "Are you ready?"

Jennifer locked her eyes on him. Just the sight of him warmed her. It was an inexplicable feeling that captivated her. She felt the urge to hold him, to play with him, to protect him. "Okay. Let's go!"

He reached for her hand. She looked down and smiled uncertainly before taking it. The little man pulled her to the edge of the hill, where sleds and riders lay perched in their snow gear, looking like little gargoyles, steely gazes focused on the expansive scene before them.

"I'll sit in front and you can sit behind me," the boy instructed.

He nudged the sled forward, sat and waited for Jennifer. She craned her neck and ventured a look down the long hill, with its furrows, slopes and dips. It was steep, and stretched out into the distant darkness of Central Park, beyond the distant park lights.

"It's a long ride," Jennifer said. "Where are your parents?"

"Are you afraid?"

Jennifer lifted her eyebrows. "Well… no… but…"

"Come on. Get on!" the boy commanded. "I won't make it if you don't come with me."

"What?"

"Come on!"

She gently lowered herself into the sled and arranged her legs around him, so that he could lean back and rest against her.

He looked back at her and smiled. "I'll be okay now. Are you ready?"

She nodded, apprehensive. "Okay…"

He planted his left hand into the ground and gave a little push. The sled inched forward, teetered on the edge, resistant, as if it, too, had suddenly seen the sharp slanting hill before it and was having second thoughts. The boy leaned and rocked it, relentlessly, until the sled finally inched forward and started its descent.

Jennifer held her breath as they shot off, gathering speed. She could hear cheers behind them, as if they were competing in the Olympics for a Gold Medal. The brisk wind numbed her face.

The first bump jolted them, nearly pitched them off the sled, but they managed to hold fast as they went plunging off into the night, past other sledders who had paused to watch them race by.

The boy squealed in ecstasy as he clumsily steered the sled across the snow that sparkled around them like scattered jewels. Jennifer gripped his little shoulders, teeth clenched, and observed the playful tug-of-war going on between the boy and the sled, as he struggled to change course to avoid approaching trees and mounds of blowing snow. As the sled bounced and sailed, she felt the pit-of-the-stomach sensation of free fall, and couldn't resist a smile at the dangerous exhilaration that she hadn't felt since she was a child, sledding down the winter hills of Tennessee.

There was a wild rush of adrenaline as they approached a fresh mound of snow, piled high by a snowplow. They braced for impact, then exploded into it, screaming, shooting into the air on the other side, landing hard and charging on, bodies tucked and close, snow fleeing from their bodies in wisps and spirals.

It was the thrill-ride of a lifetime. Snow, sky and speed held them in an unraveling timelessness, where old actions, inevitability and possibility coalesced and were about to collide, like whirling out-of-control planets.

They were near the bottom of the hill, now, and Central Park lay all around them in shadows and eerie movement. Then, from the corner of her eye, Jennifer spotted a beautiful silver sleigh, drawn by two chestnut horses, winding its way along a lower path. Their sled was closing in on it fast! If they didn't turn the sled, they would surely collide—with the horses or the sleigh! She heard the sleigh's ringing bells. Saw the white vapor puffing from the horses' nostrils. Saw the horses' wild eyes as the little sled charged.

"Look out!" Jennifer shouted, struggling to grab the rope to yank the sled away from the crash. The boy was confused and frightened.

With her right foot, Jennifer kicked the right steering bar as hard as she could. The sled jerked left, bulleted past a bank of dark trees, perilously close to the path of the sleigh. She gave the steering bar another hard kick, then wrapped her arms tightly around the boy, pulling him in close to her and enclosing him. At all costs, she had to protect him! Even if it meant losing her life, she had to protect the boy!

The sled rocketed past the sleigh, just missing the horses' front hooves. Alarmed, the horses whinnied. Their front legs kicked high into the air.

A 3-foot drop-off lay directly in the sled's path. Jennifer was helpless to avoid it. She braced, arms tightly wrapping the boy. The sled sailed, dropped and struck the ground, hard. It bounced and went spiraling out of control.

Jennifer clasped the boy firmly, as they spun off wildly into the chaotic night.

# CHAPTER 11

Jennifer's eyes flashed open, bold and scared. She was in the dark, lying in snow, shivering, shocked by the cold. She sat up, throwing darting glances, slapping the snow from her back and legs. Where was she? What had happened?

In a sudden flash, she remembered the sled ride! The near-miss collision with the sleigh, and the boy! She jumped up, blinking fast. She was alone in a light snowfall, under a cluster of trees, snow banked high to her right.

She glanced around anxiously, searching for reason and reality. Perplexed and freezing, she set off to look for the boy and the sled. She re-examined the area. She circled the trees, scanning the hill they'd just descended, but it was quiet now. No sleds! No kids! Nothing! Not a trace! Just silence.

She placed her hands on her hips and shouted, "Hello! Hello… Little boy! Anybody! Hello!? Where's the boy?" she asked aloud, hearing her voice swallowed by the endless night. She shook her head in a slow wonder, unsure what to do. Call the police? And tell them what?

One thing was clear: she needed to get out of the cold. She was shivering! She saw distant lights. She gave the area a final, thorough search, and then reluctantly trudged off toward the lights, crunching through the snow with tingling toes, damp stringy hair and wobbly legs. She wrapped her arms tightly around herself for warmth, still confused as to what had happened and where the child was. She was so cold! Her teeth chattered.

She spotted a path. Hopeful now, she scrabbled up a narrow slope, reaching the path with straining effort. She planted herself firmly on the snow-covered path and stamped the snow from her boots. Struggling for direction and clarity, she hurried along under the amber glow of park lights. Ahead, bathed in a soft yellow light, she saw stone steps climbing toward the street. She passed a final glance over her shoulder to see if the boy was there. Eerie shadows moved in the wind. She took the stairs, puffing out clouds of vapor, her throat dry, her chest heaving.

Out of dim night, Jennifer emerged onto the lighted sidewalk. People passed but they didn't seem to notice her. They stepped by her, around her, lowering their nervous eyes, mumbling back at her. She looked down at her clothes. She looked a mess! She looked like a street person! No wonder people ignored her.

Yellow cabs and limousines passed. She hailed a cab; it rushed by, spraying snow. She leapt away, shaking from cold. She flagged another cab, but it shot ahead, horn blaring. Jennifer cursed it.

Disoriented, she turned in place, on the verge of tears. What had happened? What was going on!? Where was she? She was in some kind of nightmare and she couldn't wake up!

Her only goal was to escape from the punishing cold. She had to get out of the cold. Now! She darted across the street, edging toward midtown, desperate to duck into the first shop she came to, hoping to warm herself. She'd make up her mind what to do then.

Peter S Hair Salon was the first store that came into view. She passed the full-length window and caught a glimpse of herself in the reflection of the glass.

"Oh, my God!" she whispered, horrified by her appearance. She had the face and hair of a witch! Too cold to care, she pushed open the door and entered, a wistful, wearied creature embarrassed by her shabby appearance.

The warm breath of the heat soothed and relaxed her. She exhaled tension and fear, standing near the door, rubbing her arms and stamping her ice-cold feet. Gradually, as if waking from sleep, she began taking in the shop's Christmas decorations: a small tapered Christmas tree, several red poinsettias, and green wreaths with blinking white lights and ruby red ornaments.

A sensual blue-haired receptionist, about 25 years old, with a dramatic crinkly hairstyle, stood watchful at a shiny metallic podium. She gave Jennifer the once-over, and her eyes enlarged in concern and surprise. "You look a bit stunned," the young woman said. "Are you all right?"

She was dressed in black—tight black everything—and it all clung provocatively to her yoga-esque thin body. But the single red scarf tied stylishly about her neck matched her glossy red lipstick, and was surely meant to suggest an inclination to blend her own dark style with the color of Christmas. Her practiced sophistication was aided by polished speech that made Jennifer self-conscious of her own slight Southern accent.

"Yes… just very cold."

Three hair stylists, also dressed in black, turned in unison, and viewed Jennifer curiously. The single woman stylist had short platinum blond hair and copper eyeliner that suggested a love of the nightlife. The two men looked nothing alike: one had short shocking red hair and, the other, blond shoulder-length locks that reminded Jennifer of old photos of General Custer.

When Jennifer stepped forward, the young receptionist took a step backwards.

Jennifer cleared her throat, desperate for a place to warm up. "I just need…"

The receptionist cut her off, "Yes, ma'am, I can see that," she said, lifting an eyebrow. "Well… Congratulations…," she said, uncertainly. She called to the three hairstylists. "This is it! She's the winner!"

She turned back to Jennifer, explaining. "Since you are the five thousandth customer to come in since the salon opened, you can receive a free hairstyle, courtesy of Peter S Salons, and a new designer evening dress, courtesy of Tony Este Fashions. Merry Christmas!"

Jennifer opened her mouth to speak, but nothing came out except, "Do you have anything hot to drink? Coffee, tea, anything?"

The receptionist scratched her head. "Okay… Sure. You don't have to have your hair done now. You can come back some other time, as long as it's in the next month."

Jennifer was grateful for the shelter, still chilled to the bone. "No, now is fine."

The receptionist led her to a chair and Jennifer collapsed into it, happy to sit. A moment later, the receptionist returned with a red mug of hot coffee and an almond croissant. Jennifer took them thankfully and held the steaming mug up to her face, beginning a slow descent into relaxation and warmth. She ate the croissant hastily, surprised by her hunger, and she had almost drained her mug of coffee when her hair stylist appeared.

Dale Bailey had a touch of baby-cheeked deadpan innocence that was disarming, and the reddest hair Jennifer had ever seen. He examined her carefully, assiduously, studying her face, hairline and eyes.

"I think I can do something here…but you've got to leave it all to me. No Ifs, ands or buts, and definitely, no arguments! No, 'but the last time', and, No, and I stress, with big capital letters, NO suggestions!"

Jennifer turned. "I usually just have it trimmed on top and…"

He threw up a hand. "Stop right there! What did I just say!? NO! Leave it to me. You, girl, need something entirely new! Trust me when I tell you! NEW is the word!"

Jennifer shifted, uncomfortably. "New?"

"You're not from New York, are you?" Dale asked.

"No, I'm not."

"Where are you from?"

"I don't know, really. I don't really know where I'm from anymore."

"Well, you sound like a New Yorker. Most New Yorkers aren't from New York, and, after they've been here awhile, they forget where in the hell they came from. It's that kind of place."

Before beginning, Dale grabbed a digital camera and took a "before" picture, which would be hung in the Salon, along with an "after" picture. Then he sent her to have her hair washed.

When she returned to his chair, he went to work, snipping, patting and fussing.

"Were you in a snowball fight?"

"Actually, I was sledding…with a little boy."

"Your son?"

"No."

"A friend's boy?"

"No."

"How old?"

"I don't know."

"Where is he?"

"I haven't any idea."

Dale nodded, looking at her with prying eyes. "You've just got to tell me how you wound up in New York, girl. Mysterious clients always enhance my creativity."

"If I told you, you wouldn't believe me."

"Try me."

Without any hesitation, knowing that he wouldn't believe her anyway, Jennifer felt brave enough to tell him. "Mrs. Frances Wintergreen sent me."

Dale turned his face away from her to the mirror, pondering her answer. "Hummm. You know, it's funny you should say that. About a week ago, a woman came in, and she gave me a little present."

He leaned over to the counter in front of them and, next to the styling gel, was a little snow globe. "This," he said, holding it up to the light.

Jennifer studied it, thinking it looked strangely familiar. "May I hold it?" she asked.

He handed it over. Her eyes widened in recognition. It was Harvey's Pond, in Willowbury! She saw the ice skaters, the gazebo and even the pine and fir trees surrounding it! It was an exact replication!

Jennifer twisted around toward him. "Why did she give you this?"

"I told her I wanted to buy my own place, but I couldn't afford a place in the City. Just before she left, she opened her bag and handed it to me. She said that I would live near that pond someday. She said that's where I would open my shop—in the town where that pond is."

Jennifer stared into the void, her eyes not really focusing. "Did she say what her name was?"

"No, but I looked it up in the reservation book. Frances Wintergreen."

Jennifer closed her eyes and slumped down into the chair. Dale leaned over.

"Are you okay?"

Jennifer nodded, numbly. "Oh sure... yeah, I'm just fine."

"Good. Well, don't worry, when I'm finished with you, you'll be the hottest-looking chick in New York!"

"What time is it?" Jennifer asked.

"Almost 6:30."

Jennifer dozed off. When she woke up, Dale was blow-drying her hair. Her eyes opened broadly, and she stared back at herself in the mirror, in disbelief.

Dale shouted. "Close your eyes! I'm not finished yet!"

She obeyed.

"You also need some makeup. I'm going to help you."

"But…"

He cut her off. "NO BUTS! I'm in charge here!"

Jennifer eased back while Dale reached for a conveniently placed makeup kit. "I also do makeup for a theatre company," Dale said, proudly. "When I'm finished, you are going to be camera-ready, girl."

Jennifer squeezed her eyes together tightly, trying not to be nervous, as he plucked her brows, put foundation on her face, lined her eyelids, blushed her cheeks and applied lipstick.

When he'd finished, he stepped back, folded his thick, genie-like arms and told her to open her eyes. She did.

"Well, what do you think?"

She saw layers and curls, gleaming under the light. There was a fullness and body to the style—a magnificent sheen! She touched her hair carefully, as if it were a brand new object. Her face looked buffed and soft, cheek bones highlighted, eyes glamorous. She actually looked mysterious! Imagine her, looking glamorous and mysterious!

Dale looked on proudly. "Not bad, huh? So, what do you think?" he barked, impatiently.

Jennifer sat up. "I don't know… I mean, I've never seen myself look like this."

"Of course you haven't, because you were working at *ugly*, girl. UGLY! And you're not! You've got a nice face, nice body and nice hair. But, and I stress *but*, it was a mess! I don't know who's been cutting your hair, but in my opinion, you should sue for malpractice and fire that chick or dude!"

Jennifer looked at Dale in wonder. "You're a real artist."

Dale beamed. "Yep, I can't deny it. I'm a regular genius."

After Dale showed her off, demanding compliments and applause, he escorted her next door to Tony Este Fashions.

There, Dale introduced her to Cheryl, a woman of 35 who had a willowy figure, large brown eyes and short amber hair. She made a quick study of Jennifer and then excused herself to the back room, while Dale continued making minor adjustments to Jennifer's makeup and hair.

A moment later, Cheryl reappeared beaming. She presented a golden satin dress with spaghetti straps, a hidden back zipper and back slit. She brought matching shoes: golden satin sling backs, with a rhinestone trim.

Jennifer eyed them, worried. "You think so?" she asked.

Both Cheryl and Dale nodded. "Made for you," Cheryl said, with a firm conviction. "Trust me."

Ten minutes later, Jennifer was parading in front of the full-length mirror, moving languidly; the dress had somehow given her new grace and form. She felt strange, as if she were hovering just above ground, like an object from another planet, unsure if the ground would support her when she landed. Her eyes shifted from the mirror to Cheryl and Dale, who looked on with serious analytical stares and posed bodies.

"You look tense," Dale said.

"I am!"

"Throw back your head in a carefree manner," Dale instructed.

"How do I do that?"

Dale screwed up his lips in irritation. "Like this!" he said, demonstrating.

She tried it, watching the lines fade from her face, watching her hair bounce. Her furrowed brow disappeared. She looked younger, prettier. She grinned. "It worked!" she said, surprised.

"Of course it worked," Dale said. "I know what I'm doing, girl!"

"Now you have celebrity wattage," Cheryl said.

Dale danced around her, snapping "after" pictures.

"Your boyfriend's going to love your new look," Cheryl said.

"Where is he taking you tonight?" Dale asked.

Jennifer's palms moistened. She remembered the child's words to her just before they took the sled ride. *"You'll meet him soon,"* he had said.

"I don't know. I don't have a boyfriend."

"I have a brother," Cheryl said. "Nice looking. He just broke up with his girlfriend and I know he'd love to take you out on the town."

Jennifer looked over. "No… thanks."

"Are you going to wear it, or shall I wrap it for you?" Cheryl asked.

Jennifer's eyes were suddenly drawn to a newspaper that was lying on a table nearby. She crossed to it and picked it up. It was open to the second page; the headline caught her eye:

**CHRISTMAS EVE MIRACLE**
**BOY RETURNS TO LIFE AFTER SLEDDING ACCIDENT**

When she saw the photograph, she was stunned. It was the boy! The same boy who had been leading her around! The same boy she had gone sledding with!

She dropped down into the nearest chair, her face blank with shock.

Cheryl went over. "What's the matter?"

Jennifer couldn't find words. She anxiously read the article.

*A six-year-old boy, who had been pronounced dead on arrival at Mercy Hospital after a sledding accident in Central*

*Park, began breathing again twenty minutes later. His father was by his bedside when he suddenly noticed the child begin to breathe. Doctors were quickly summoned, and by the time they arrived, the child was sitting up in bed, asking for a soda.*

*After a thorough examination, it was determined that the trauma to the child's head had miraculously disappeared and, except for a few cuts and bruises, he was in perfect health. The doctors were at a loss to explain the sudden change; however, the child maintains that he was saved by a Christmas Angel, who was with him on the sled and protected him when the sled went out of control and struck a tree.*

Jennifer slowly lifted her eyes from the newspaper to Dale's and Cheryl's curious faces. She gave them a strange and vivid stare. "I don't understand what is happening to me. I don't understand how time could have passed like this."

Their faces held concern and sorrow, but they didn't speak.

Jennifer shot up. "Where is Mercy Hospital?"

# CHAPTER 12

At the hospital information desk, Jennifer quickly explained whom she wanted to see. She was asked to sign in and then given the room number.

Inside the elevator, she pressed 7 and stepped back, clutching the Tony Este bag Cheryl had placed her old clothes in, and a brown teddy bear she'd purchased at the hospital gift shop. She wasn't sure what to expect: whether it would really be the same child, whether the child would even recognize her or what would happen if he did recognize her.

She stepped hesitantly out of the elevator and made her way down the gray tiled hallway, past a Christmas tree and open doors where TVs played holiday classic movies and parents lingered in doorways with faces of concern and apprehension. Nurses passed and smiled, while aides pushed carts and bantered about Christmas shopping. Jennifer took off her coat and draped it over her arm as she continued on, smelling a combination of coffee and rubbing alcohol, until she located the boy's room. She paused, hearing Charlie Brown's voice coming from the television inside, and recognized the program as *A Charlie Brown Christmas*. A young, blond, Hollywood-handsome doctor exited the room, stopped mid-stride, and looked Jennifer over approvingly. Slowly, he continued down the corridor, twisting back for an extravagant final glance before turning the corner. She looked down at herself self-consciously, wishing now that she'd taken the time to change clothes and have Cheryl box up the new dress.

Still unsure, she ventured inside the room, noticing a child's playful scribbles of Christmas trees and Santas taped to the walls. A toy kangaroo with a baby in her pouch stood guard at the foot of the bed. More stuffed animals lay beneath a miniature Christmas tree; and get-well cards and Christmas cards were displayed on the windowsill.

When Jennifer saw him, she froze. It was the same child—the same child she had sledded with! He was propped up in bed, dressed in red pajamas, with crayons scattered carelessly around him. He was immersed in drawing a new masterpiece.

When he looked up and their eyes met, his face came alive, as if he'd just seen Santa Claus. He squealed, ecstatic, dropped his crayons and went to Jennifer in a rush. She dropped her bag and, instinctively, opened her arms. He leapt into them.

"I'm so glad you're all right," Jennifer said, embracing him. "I didn't know what happened to you."

The child pulled back briefly to study her. "You look different," the child said. "Better!"

"I feel better!" Jennifer said, hugging him again.

At the same moment, the young and startling handsome doctor reappeared with a middle-aged nurse. They took in the scene, exchanged puzzled glances, and went over.

"It's the angel!" the child yelled. "It's the angel I told you about! She was with me! She was with me on the sled!"

Jennifer felt the warmth of the child's body as she held him; felt him squirm and twist toward the doctor and nurse. She was a little embarrassed, but pleased. It felt so natural to hold him, to smell his sweet candy breath, to feel the immense pleasure of being connected and close.

The doctor and nurse waited for an explanation, but Jennifer ignored them for a moment and put her full attention on the child.

"I was so worried," Jennifer said.

She could feel eyes on her. It seemed dangerous, somehow, to say more than that. She didn't know what had really happened. She didn't really know who this child was.

"See," the boy said to the doctor and nurse, "I told you she was real!"

The doctor said, "So you did, Jason. So you did."

Jennifer finally released the boy, and sat him on the edge of the bed so that his legs dangled. She presented him with the teddy bear. "He reminded me of you," Jennifer said.

Jason took the bear and hugged it, gleefully. "It's mine!"

"Yes, Jason," Jennifer said, "It's all yours!"

The doctor approached and extended his hand. "I'm Dr. Phillips. Dr. Hal Phillips, and this is Nurse Flanders," he said, looking toward the nurse.

Jennifer studied him for a moment, and at first sight, she thought he had the innocence and wholesome look of a minister, with his blond hair and blue eyes. But, on closer examination, she saw there were things that betrayed that image: mischievous eyebrows and a devious glint of expectation and desire in his eyes.

Jennifer took his hand, limply. "I'm Jennifer Taylor."

Dr. Phillips' eyes wandered over her, as though she were a dessert tray. Jennifer's eyes slid away from him, following Nurse Flanders, who went over to Jason and asked to see his new teddy bear.

"So are you a friend of the family?" the doctor asked.

Jennifer quickly analyzed the question. She thought it might be best if she said she was; it would make perfect sense and there might be fewer questions to answer. "Yes, I'm sort of a friend."

The nurse helped Jason back to his pillow and crayons. His little face scrunched up in confusion. "You're not our friend. You're an angel."

Jennifer chuckled, nervously. "Well, yes, I mean, some in the family think I'm kind of an angel. I mean, I help out when I can."

The doctor took another appetizing look at her. "Well, Jennifer, if I may call you Jennifer, you certainly look like an angel."

Obviously, Nurse Flanders had heard it all before, and she rolled her eyes toward the ceiling.

"So, does that mean you and Alex are good friends?" Dr. Phillips asked.

Jennifer swallowed. "Alex?"

Dr. Phillips crossed his arms. "Yes, Jason's father."

"Oh, Alex! You mean, Alex?"

"Yes."

Jennifer shifted her weight. "Well, yes, we're good friends…Alex and I...Yes, we've been friends for…oh, yeah, for a while, now."

Jason spoke up. "You have?"

Jennifer turned to him, folding her hands tightly, her eyes shifting anxiously. "Yes, Jason, you know that."

"But my Daddy didn't believe me when I told him about you," Jason said.

Jennifer laughed, awkwardly. "Your father's just teasing you, Jason."

Dr. Phillips said, "Well, Alex should be here any minute."

Jennifer faced him, alarmed. "Really?"

Dr. Phillips looked at his watch. "Yes, he left to get a few things for Jason. He called just a minute ago. Said he was on his way."

Jennifer nodded, rapidly, struggling to think. She looked at Jason. "I should probably be going."

Jason sank, disappointed. "Don't leave. You just came. I want my Daddy to see you, because he didn't believe me."

"Yes, Jason, but now Dr. Phillips has seen me and he will tell your father that I exist. I mean, your Daddy knows I exist."

"You look dressed for a night out, Jennifer," Dr. Phillips said. "A Christmas Eve party?"

It gave her an idea. "Yes… And, I'm late. I've really got to be going. People are waiting…"

"Don't go!" Jason called out. "My Daddy… he doesn't believe me! He doesn't believe that you're an angel!"

Jennifer went to him, and eased down on the edge of the bed next to him. "Jason, I'm just a woman, and I was so lucky to have met you. But I'm not an angel."

Jennifer's back was to the door and she didn't notice when Alex and Valencia entered the room. Jason didn't notice either.

"But you were there with me on the sled," Jason said. "You kept it from hitting that sleigh."

"Yes, I was with you, but you wanted me to follow you, remember? You asked me to take the sled ride with you."

"But you steered the sled away from the sleigh and you held me when we hit that tree so that it didn't hurt. You did! Don't you remember?"

"I remember holding you, Jason, but I'm not an angel."

"Who are you, then?" Alex asked.

Jennifer spun around and saw a tall man of perhaps 30 looking back at her. He wore a dark leather jacket, blue jeans and black cowboy boots. He stood firmly, with his barrel chest lifted, in a stance that was strong but not threatening. His dark hair was long, stylishly unruly, combed back from his smooth forehead, revealing a broad handsome face and sharp jaw-line.

There was a subdued charisma about him. His dark prowling eyes startled her. There was a remote fire in them that seemed clouded by worries and concerns. As his eyes held her for a long private moment, she didn't run from his gaze, which surprised her, even while she felt the heat of embarrassment rise to her face for staring back so long.

Jennifer gradually became aware of the woman standing next to him, who in her middle or late 20s, had the luster of wealth and privilege about her. It showed in her aloof, aristocratic face, the confidence in her expression, the expensive full-length cashmere coat and dangling diamond earrings. Her hair was richly long and blond, her lips full, denim blue eyes watchful and narrowed, as if perceiving a threat.

All the eyes in the room were on Jennifer: Jason's, Alex's, Valencia's, Dr. Phillips' and Nurse Flanders'.

Dr. Phillips turned to Alex and said, flippantly, "She said she's a family friend."

Jennifer stood slowly, and became surprisingly aware that the dress helped give her poise and strength. Magically, she felt her chest and shoulders lift, her head rise comfortably. She looked at Alex directly, confidently. "I'm Jennifer Taylor."

In those seconds, she saw a clearing in his eyes, like dark clouds fleeing to the corners of the sky, leaving a fathomless dome of blue. They boldly looked back at her and, suddenly, she felt tremors of astonishing attraction. It took a Herculean effort for her to look away from him.

"And you were with my son on that sled?"

"Yes."

"Didn't you know that he had run away? Didn't you try to find me or Valencia? We were worried sick! We didn't know where he was or what had happened to him."

Jennifer stuttered. "I didn't know…"

"Why did you run away?"

"I didn't… I mean…I…"

Valencia interrupted. "Well, you certainly weren't around when the people from the sleigh arrived. If you were with Jason, then why did you run away? Why didn't you help him?" she asked, accusingly.

Jennifer struggled to come up with an answer, but knew that whatever she said wouldn't make any sense, so she didn't even try.

"She did help me!" Jason yelled. "She did! She saved me! She saved me!"

Nurse Flanders lowered her head and left the room. Dr. Phillips remained, enjoying the drama.

Alex laid the little suitcase down next to Valencia, and started toward his son, gently brushing Jennifer. When they touched—which was ever so slightly, the brush of his left arm against hers—they both felt an unexpected heat arise from an unknown place deep within, and with it, a sharp, rapid recognition of familiarity and longing. He paused for only seconds in that mystery of vulnerability and excitement, then went to Jason.

Jennifer was short of breath. Just standing still, watching him lift his son into his arms, made her short of breath!

"It's all right, Jason," he said, smoothly, giving him a playful hug. "Everything is great now that you're okay. We're going to eat pizza, go to movies and…"

"… But you don't believe me!" Jason said.

Alex held him at arm's length. "Of course I believe you, J-boy!"

"Then tell Jennifer you believe her."

Alex lowered his head, then turned to Jennifer. "I believe you," he said, flatly.

Jason made an ugly face.

Alex tried again. "Ms. Taylor, if Jason says you're an angel, then I believe you're an angel."

"Alex," Valencia said, sharply, "I hate to remind you, but we have some last minute Christmas shopping to do."

Alex turned to her reluctantly, consciously avoiding Jennifer. "I don't think I can leave J-boy."

"But we have a hundred things to do before we go to my parents' party at nine o'clock," she continued, looking directly at Jennifer.

"Don't go yet, Daddy," Jason pleaded. "Please!"

"We'll be back in a few hours, Jason," Valencia said. "Just a few hours."

Jason ignored her. "Please, Daddy…"

Alex tapped his son's nose, playfully, and looked at Valencia. "Why don't you go ahead, Valencia? I'll catch up with you a little later."

The room turned quiet. Valencia gave Alex a cool gaze, then put her full attention on Jason, forcing a sweet tone that came out mildly strident. "Jason will be fine, won't you, Jason? You're a big boy, now."

Jason shook his head, sadly. "I'm not that big. I'm just a kid."

Alex said, "I need to stay here awhile, Valencia. Really… You go ahead. J-boy and I need some time together. He's been through a lot."

Jason looked at Valencia. "Yeah, I've been through a lot!"

Valencia slowly adjusted her purse strap, then switched the purse from her right shoulder to her left, unsuccessfully suppressing an angry look. She pivoted and left.

Jennifer looked away, aware that Dr. Phillips' eyes were still on her.

"I should go," she said looking down at her watch.

"Stay with me!" Jason said.

Dr. Phillips spoke up. "Jason, you need to get some rest. You've been through quite an adventure."

Alex turned to the doctor. "Can I stay with him?"

"Of course," Dr. Phillips said. "But he should try to sleep."

"But I'm not tired!" Jason protested.

"The doctor's right, J-boy," Alex said, easing him back down onto the bed. "You need to rest."

Jason looked at Jennifer, hopefully, reaching for the teddy bear she brought him. "You'll come back, won't you, Jennifer?"

Jennifer hesitated. "I'll try."

"Promise me," Jason said.

She smiled. "Okay, Jason, I promise I'll come back."

Alex stole a quick glance at Jennifer, and their eyes met again, briefly. Jennifer drew an inconspicuous breath, to cool herself down, then started toward the door.

As she was leaving the room, she heard Jason say to his father, "Go with her, Daddy! Go with Jennifer!"

In the hallway, she walked toward the elevators, but stopped when Dr. Phillips called for her and hurried over.

"Look, I'm out of here in an hour or so. How about dinner or something?"

Jennifer looked back toward Jason's room, feeling a heaviness in her chest, a strange feeling that she was leaving a part of herself behind. "I don't think so, Dr. Phillips."

"Someone waiting for you at the party?"

"No… no one is waiting for me."

"Wow, I find that hard to believe, Jennifer. You know, I sense something about you."

"Really?"

"Yeah… I sense that you're about to make the biggest decision of your life."

She perked up. "What do you mean?"

"I'm not sure really. Call it a doctor's intuition. The first time I saw you, I said to myself, what a great time we could have together—I mean, a truly great time, even awesome. Don't ask me why, it's just one of those strong feelings, and you can ask anyone around here, I'm not one of those people who has these kinds of rash and sudden feelings. I'm logical, practical and generally dependable, not given to quick and irrational decisions. However, in your case, I'm making an exception and, I must admit, I'm completely baffled as to why."

Jennifer stared at him, suspiciously, seeing Nurse Flanders out of the corner of her eye, shaking her head.

"No thanks, doctor," she said, smiling weakly.

He shrugged. "I'm not bad to look at, am I?"

"No. Not bad at all."

"I have a great career, a beautiful duplex apartment here in the city, and a home in Bridgehampton. I also know where all the best parties are. You would have a wonderful Christmas."

Jennifer looked at him frankly. "And what happens after Christmas?"

He stuffed his hands into his white jacket pockets. "We'd cross that bridge when we came to it. No promises, but a hell of a good time."

Jennifer turned toward the elevator, seeing two doors. It occurred to her, inexplicably, that she *was* about to make a decision that would affect the rest of her life and, as weird as that seemed, she was suddenly terrified.

Dr. Phillips could see she was vulnerable. "We'd have an adventure together, and I guarantee you wouldn't regret it. I know how to make women very happy," he said, with a confident grin.

Jennifer was about to walk away when she saw Alex watching her from the doorway of Jason's room. It was unnerving. Two men—two attractive men—were looking at her longingly. She had never thought of herself as being particularly attractive. For most of her life, she'd defined herself by what Lance had thought of her: how he reacted to her thoughts, her clothes, her make-up, her actions. After his death, there was no need to be pretty or attractive—there was no need to waste thoughts on clothes or makeup or having a family. There was no room for any of them in her life.

She swung into her coat. As she stared into Dr. Phillips' face, searching for an answer, she saw Alex approach from the corner of her eye. When she turned to him, he had a peculiar look on his face.

## CHAPTER 13

Jennifer, Dr. Phillips and Alex all stood awkwardly in the hospital corridor, while a lively orchestral version of *We Wish You a Merry Christmas* drifted in from a distant room.

"I just wanted to apologize for what I said back there," Alex said. "It's just that I was so worried when he ran away," he continued, running his fingers through his thick hair. "And then when we found him like that, unconscious…"

"How did you find him?" Jennifer asked.

"Whenever J-boy and I go out, I always make sure he's wearing a little identification tag and chain around his neck with my name, cell number and home number on it. People in the sleigh found the tag and called me before the ambulance took him to the hospital."

"When had you noticed he was missing?"

"At F.A.O. Schwartz. We were together one minute, then I just looked around and he was gone."

"I wish I could explain it all," Jennifer said. "But…"

Dr. Phillips crossed his arms. "I'm just curious, Jennifer. What happened to you after the sled struck the tree?"

Jennifer stared, thoughtfully. "I don't know. Maybe I hit my head or something. When I woke up, I was alone. I looked for Jason everywhere, but he was gone."

"You must have wandered off somehow. Don't you think you should be examined?" Dr. Phillips asked.

"No… I'm fine."

"You should have an examination," he said, lifting a gleaming eye.

"No, I'm fine, really." She paused and looked directly into Dr. Phillips' eyes. "So was Jason really… dead?"

He nodded.

"For how long?"

"About twenty minutes," Dr. Phillips said. "It's kind of a miracle."

The elevator door opened and Jennifer looked over. "I should go."

Dr. Phillips stepped toward her, took out a business card and handed it to her. "Like I said, I'm off in an hour. Call me."

Jennifer took it, reluctantly, gave Alex a last look and hurried into the elevator, seconds before the double doors closed behind her. As the elevator descended to the lobby, she twisted her hands restlessly. Her stomach was in knots. When she closed her eyes, all she saw was Alex's face.

After the elevator door opened, she rearranged her bags and walked briskly through the lobby, hearing her heels click across the floor. She needed to get to the front door. She needed air. But as she walked, the double glass doors seemed to move farther and farther away. Something had happened when she'd looked into Alex's eyes. It was as if the two of them had connected in an ineffable way. As a result, some deep-seated fear in her had been released from its cage and was snapping at her heels like an angry dog.

Outside, the air was cool and damp. She let the snow fall in her hair and on her shoulders while she allowed herself to take some deep breaths. All about her was shimmering winter, pressing crowds and restless traffic. Just as she was beginning to relax, she heard Alex's deep voice behind her, a rich voice that sang with strength and sensuality.

"Do you want to share a cab?"

She didn't turn. "Ah… No, thanks, I'm going to walk."

He came up alongside her. "In those shoes? They look expensive."

"No, not really. They're not really expensive at all... well maybe they are."

"But aren't your feet cold in them?"

"Cold?" she asked, looking down at them, definitely cold. "No… no, my feet seldom ever get cold."

He stared doubtfully, pocketing his hands. "J-boy, I mean, Jason, commanded me to come after you to thank you. He threw me out of his room."

"You did thank me."

"Well, yes… Have you got time for coffee or something?"

"I'm a… well, I'm supposed to…"

"I don't know what happened on that sled, but I do know that Jason is alive and he says you're the reason. Please, let me at least buy you a cup of coffee."

"Aren't you supposed to meet your fiancée or something?"

"She's shopping. She won't mind. So… coffee?"

Jennifer fully intended to say no. "All right…"

"I know a great little place up on West 70th Street."

In the taxi, they were both silent. Jennifer watched the many lights of Christmas drift by, feeling a persistent drumming in her chest. Alex kept a good two-foot distance between them, as he gazed absently out the opposite window, his fingers drumming on his right leg.

"Have you been in New York long?" he finally asked.

"No," Jennifer said, seeing his reflection looking at her in her window.

On the radio, Bing Crosby sang *White Christmas.*

"Do you have family in New York?" Alex asked.

"No."

"Are you visiting friends?"

"No."

"Are you here alone?"

Jennifer waited. "Yes."

"A vacation?"

"No."

"Business?"

She finally turned to him, forcing a smile. "Are you an attorney?"

He laughed nervously. "Oh, yeah… the 50 questions. I'm sorry. I guess I'm a little tense and when I'm tense, I ask a lot of questions."

She let her eyes linger on his timid smile and moist lips. Her right foot began to jiggle. "That's okay."

They entered Café Pierre. A hostess seated them at a table looking out onto 70th Street. Alex helped Jennifer out of her coat as she took in the elegant café—its photographs and paintings of New York City street scenes, an old grand piano and a large glass-enclosed dessert display.

By the time they were seated and had received their menus, a pianist began playing *The Moonlight Sonata.*

Alex looked up from his menu. "Who wrote that piece? Mozart?"

Jennifer listened. "No, Beethoven, I think… The only reason I know is that I had a boyfriend who loved Beethoven. He loved music."

"What happened to him?"

Jennifer put her nose back into the menu. "He died a year ago."

He spoke in a near whisper. "I'm so sorry."

They studied their menus, listening to the music. The melody took Jennifer back to quiet evenings in Tennessee, when she and Lance had prepared dinner and listened to music. She'd often thought of it as an irritating intrusion. She was even a little jealous of it, because Lance's attention often strayed from the topics of office politics and spreadsheet short cuts to the sounds of Bach, Beethoven or Duke Ellington. His eyes took on a faraway distracted stare, as if he were entranced, and he absently contributed to the conversation with an occasional "Really" or "I see."

"Did you know that Beethoven didn't name that piece *The Moonlight Sonata*?" Jennifer asked.

Alex looked up. "No, I didn't."

"A music critic wrote that the sonata reminded him of moonlight reflected off a lake or something like that. So a publisher gave it the name, because he thought it would sell more copies. As it turned out, it did. It became the all-time best-selling piece of sheet music during that time. The publisher was a good businessman."

"Yes, I would think so. Your boyfriend told you that story?"

"Yes… I hadn't even thought about it until now. I'm surprised I remembered. I guess I admired the publisher's business savvy and it stuck in my head."

"Are you a good businesswoman?" Alex asked.

Jennifer feigned modesty. "I think so."

Alex studied her. "An entrepreneur?"

"Until recently."

Jennifer ignored the menu and listened carefully to the music. It was as if she were hearing the piece for the first time. It didn't sadden her as it often had in the past; on the contrary, she felt comforted and soothed by it.

Jennifer felt Alex's eyes on her as she listened. She liked his one-pointed stare, the little furrow on his brow, his smile, tentative and reflective. She had coyly stolen quick looks into his searching dark eyes, and she saw a tinge of sorrow in them that added to his attractiveness.

When the piece quietly ended, her eyes had misted with tears.

"You must have been very close to him," Alex said, softly.

She reached into her purse, drew out a tissue and gently blotted her eyes. "I'm sorry…Where did that come from?"

"Don't apologize. I understand what it's like to lose someone you love."

"It's strange, you know. For the first time in a year, I feel like I can almost let go of him."

Alex felt the impulse to reach for her hand, but he didn't. They stared at each other for a moment then, awkwardly, they avoided each other's eyes, only to finally give in, drawn by an insistent hope and a remarkable attraction.

They ordered coffee, a cannoli and a cheesecake. Jennifer was hungry, so she also ordered a grilled chicken sandwich. After the waitress left, they both eased back in their chairs, unsure of what to say or do next.

The pianist started playing a lively variation on *Jingle Bells* and the room came to life. Cheerful faces peeked out over laptops and from behind newspapers; even the waiters and waitresses stopped to pay attention and tap their feet. As the music danced and leapt about the room, Jennifer brightened, gently tapping her fingers to the rhythm. She glanced at Alex and, when he smiled back at her, a searing heat rose to her face. She was stunned by it, so she held herself utterly still, afraid that moving would shatter the magical spell and plunge her right back into the all too-familiar reality of darkness, confusion and pain.

When the pianist's hands bounced off the final chord, his head snapped back dramatically, and the room erupted in applause. Jennifer and Alex joined in, buoyant.

Moments later, the coffee, sandwich and desserts arrived. Jennifer picked up her knife to cut her cannoli into two pieces, then stopped and watched Alex surgically divide his cheesecake into two equal parts. He presented her his plate. "Want half?"

She scratched her cheek and smiled, as she cut the cannoli in two and slid half over into his plate. He did the same thing, grinning into the table.

"Just like we've known each other for years," Alex said, his eyes shining brightly.

Jennifer avoided his eyes and remained silent as she took a bite of her sandwich.

"How long will you be in town?" Alex asked.

"I don't know."

"Why did you come?"

"It was a gift."

"Really. From whom?"

"Are you sure you're not an attorney?" she asked, amused.

Alex grinned. "Funny you should ask. I'm starting law school next month."

Jennifer nodded firmly, impressed. "A law degree is a good degree to have. You can always find a well-paying job with a law degree. You have so many more options for careers."

"Yes," Alex said, unenthusiastically.

"You don't seem very excited about it."

"History and literature are my first loves."

"What can you do with history, except maybe teach, and there's no money in that," Jennifer said.

He looked at her, strangely. "That's true, but I sure did love it. Not that it was ever easy—kids are so damn complicated, but I love seeing the sparks in their eyes when something grabs them: an idea or an event, or some historical figure like Teddy Roosevelt or Abigail Adams. It's so much fun watching them work and grow with an idea. You don't get them all, of course, but that's also a fun challenge. You keep refining and working your techniques."

Jennifer kept passing glances toward the pianist. She saw the pleasurable expression on his face, as if he had found his secret to living. He was connecting completely and joyfully to life. People around him looked on with admiration and contentment and she, herself, felt enriched and gladdened by the music and the celebratory atmosphere that it was helping to create. She slowly turned back to Alex.

"You get excited when you talk about teaching. I see the sparks in your eyes, just the way you spoke about the kids when an idea grabs them." She took a beat, surprising herself with her audacity. "What do you want, Alex? What do you really want to do with your life?"

His face opened, suddenly buoyant and young. "I loved teaching."

Jennifer straightened, and when she spoke, her voice held authority. "Then maybe that's what you should do. Go back to teaching. There's nothing wrong with getting a law degree, if that's what you want to do, but if you're just doing it for the money or for whatever, then I think it's a mistake."

Alex looked at her admiringly. "Over the last two years, I've worked as a waiter and a painter… I've worked in construction, even pretended I was a cowboy for a while out in Montana…Boy, did J-boy love that! We had such great times out there! Anyway, the whole time, I kept thinking about going back to teaching, but I thought I needed to find something where I could just make a lot of money."

"I'm sure you're a wonderful teacher," Jennifer said, "and you'd probably make a good attorney."

As soon as the words left Jennifer's lips, she felt something in the back of her mind struggling to work its way forward, in recognition. It was a name or phrase, half remembered, the fragment of a conversation, lingering out on the periphery, just out of reach.

"Anything wrong?" Alex asked.

Jennifer shook it away. "No, just a feeling or something."

Jennifer took her first bite of the cheesecake and beamed in approval. "This is *so* good!"

"Your teeth are perfect," Alex observed.

Jennifer reached for coffee, a bit surprised by the comment. "Now you sound like a dentist!"

They exchanged smiles and Jennifer continued. "I had braces. My parents couldn't afford it but..."

"But?"

"Oh, nothing. I was just thinking how hard it must be to be a parent. How tough it must have been for my parents."

"Yes, it's incredibly challenging on many levels."

"Especially when you're also trying to find yourself, as my father was."

Alex hunched his shoulders, and turned reflective. "Yeah... I hope Jason doesn't grow up to hate me for what I've done—dragging him around like I did. Sometimes I wonder what the hell kind of father I've been. J-boy hasn't had a very good home."

"He knows you love him and it's obvious that he loves you."

"He's starting school now. He needs a good, stable home."

"So you'll have one soon with your fiancée."

Alex ate, distractedly. "I was hoping J-boy would warm up to Valencia, but he hasn't. That's why he ran away, because he... well, he doesn't want me to marry her."

"He probably just needs some time."

"I was worried sick," Alex continued. "I didn't know where to look or what to do. Then, after he was pronounced dead and he...came back to life, I felt like... Well, I feel like I've been given a second chance somehow. I'm starting to see things differently, more clearly. It's like I can stand outside myself and see what a fool I've been. So selfish and childish."

"You're being a little hard on yourself, aren't you?"

"No, I'm not. I've just been so confused..." He looked up at her. "Until I saw you."

Jennifer ducked her head, swallowed more cheesecake and quickly reached for her coffee. "Me?" she said quietly.

"Don't ask me why, but I'm just starting to second-guess everything."

They stared into each other's eyes, disturbed and hopeful, trying to fight the lure of attraction.

Jennifer changed the subject. "The snow's beautiful, isn't it?"

Alex didn't take his eyes from her. "I had a teacher back in high school who once told our class that we were constantly writing the story of our lives with our thoughts, words and actions. She said we were responsible for the quality and the shape of our lives. She was one of the reasons I decided to go into teaching. Her dedication and concern for her students were incredibly inspirational. I'd forgotten all about that until Jason's accident… until I saw you standing there with him."

Jennifer took another quick bite of the dessert. "When is the wedding?" she asked, trying for a casual tone.

Alex reached for his coffee, lifted the cup and then replaced it solemnly. He turned toward the window. "June…"

Jennifer lowered her eyes and was only vaguely aware that the pianist was playing *Silent Night*. "Oh," was all she could manage.

"We've both been married before. She's divorced and… my wife died about two years ago."

Jennifer sat back, stunned. "I'm so sorry… then we've both had losses."

Alex avoided her eyes. "Yes."

Jennifer waited a moment before speaking. "A June

wedding. Sounds romantic," she said, at a near whisper.

Alex reached for his coffee again and took a sip. "Yes…"

"Does Jason miss his mother?"

"Yes…"

"What was she like?"

He smiled warmly. "Full of life, generous, scattered. She was always forgetting little things: her car keys, her winter gloves, where she had put the latest book she was reading. She loved books. Usually had two or three going at once. But she was always there for Jason. Always made sure he was taken care of. She liked people and she believed in me, and in our relationship."

"She sounds very special."

"Yes, she was."

While the pianist played *Carole of the Bells*, Alex and Jennifer finished their desserts and drained their coffee cups.

"Tell me a story about a Christmas you remember when you were a little girl," Alex said.

"What do you mean?"

"What was Christmas like when you were a girl?"

Jennifer thought for a moment. "My mother worked in a factory where they put gift baskets together for special occasions, you know like Valentine's Day, Thanksgiving and Christmas. At Christmas, our little house was always filled with beautiful baskets of fruit and candies and little stuffed Santa Clauses. I was always so surprised and happy. I used to leap up and dance around the house when she brought them out and placed them on the tables and windowsills."

Alex watched her intently, his eyes sparkling.

"I found out later that those baskets were the rejects. Mama didn't have the money to buy them and my father was an alcoholic and couldn't keep a job, so… She got them half price and even then, it took her months to pay for them."

"I'd like to have met your mother," Alex said.

Jennifer closed her eyes for a moment, as if to ask again for forgiveness. "She was a good mother. I didn't realize it until recently. I only hope I can do as well, if I ever become a mother."

"You will be a wonderful mother. Is your father still alive?"

"No… he passed away two years ago." She paused, staring down at the table. "What about your parents? Are they excited about the wedding?"

"Well, we had kind of a falling out. I haven't spoken to them for a long time."

The music was rising and falling across the murmur of voices and the busy steps of the servers.

She looked up. "You should invite them to your wedding," Jennifer said. "Time goes by so fast, Alex." She stopped, realizing she'd spoken his name for the first time. It gave her a private pleasure. She continued on. "I've realized that recently. I wish, now, I hadn't shut my parents out. I wish I could take back every cruel thing I ever said."

He considered her words, folding his hands.

"They must miss Jason terribly," Jennifer added.

"Yeah… I've been thinking about that since this happened. I've been thinking I should call them." Alex looked at her deeply. "You know, I think they would like you."

When she lifted her face to meet his gaze, she saw something ignite in his eyes. She wondered if he was unraveling like she was. Did she make him feel vulnerable and powerful? Frightened and safe—every contradiction and cliché she could think of? She knew that if she let herself go, if she allowed herself to fall into that infinite moment of rapture, his eyes would melt her.

Then, just as she was about to pull her eyes from his face, the nagging thought in the back of her mind suddenly became illuminated. She should have known! She should have remembered! She *would* have remembered if she hadn't been so distracted and confused by everything that had happened! It was so obvious!

She sat up, astonished. "You're Alex Hartman!"

# CHAPTER 14

They walked slowly, silently, watching the halo of the streetlights on $70^{th}$ Street and the snow flurries falling lazily through the light, like little insects circling a flame. The five inches of snow on the ground muted the sounds of the city and made the atmosphere more intimate and private, despite the restaurants they passed, where patrons were lively and animated, and the crowds who roamed the streets with red cheeks were buoyant and cheerful.

Jennifer had changed her shoes back at the café, putting the heels in the bag with her old clothes. Alex was carrying it.

"So my father didn't send you to find me?" Alex asked.

"I told you he didn't. He doesn't even know I left town."

"And all of this is just coincidence?" Alex asked, trying to understand. "Just a coincidence that you bought the same building where Donna had a bookstore and café? A coincidence that you went on that sled ride with Jason? It's all just a coincidence? Am I supposed to believe that?"

Jennifer heard the edge in his voice. "I don't know,

Alex. I don't know anything or understand anything! Believe what you want to believe!"

Alex turned away. "I don't know what to believe about anything anymore. Everything seems so confusing. It's like I can't even think straight."

"Join the club," Jennifer said.

Alex reached for his cell phone. "I need to call J-boy."

Jennifer turned her back to him as he called and spoke playfully with Jason. There was such love in his voice—such joy!

"Yes, Jason, she's here with me… Yes… Yes… Okay, I'll tell her. You get some sleep now and I'll be back soon… Love you, J-boy."

After he replaced the phone in his jacket pocket, he faced her. "Jason said to tell you that he's sleeping with the bear you brought him."

"I'm glad he likes it."

"He likes you."

"Well, we had quite an adventure together."

"So I'd like to hear about it."

"Maybe someday…"

Alex eyed her curiously. "I don't know what to think about anything and you know what? I don't care. I don't want to think right now. Right now I just want to be a little crazy!" He looked east, suddenly getting an idea. "Go skating with me! Wollman Rink is over on 64th Street."

"Skating? But what about…?"

"Hey…it's Christmas Eve, it's snowing and we're not going to think. No more thinking and trying to figure everything out. Let's just go and have fun."

She couldn't hide her sudden pleasure. "Should we?"

"You do skate, don't you? I mean you've lived in Willowbury for almost a year. Everybody in Willowbury ice skates."

"I'm not very good."

Alex saw a taxi and hailed it. They climbed in and started for Wollman Rink. Jennifer grew excited. When the first phrases of "should not" and "what am I doing?" intruded, she pushed them out of her mind. She looked at Alex. He rubbed his hands together, eagerly.

"I haven't been ice skating since I left Willowbury."

"I'm going to have to change my clothes," Jennifer said.

"Don't worry, they have lockers."

The taxi dropped them at the curb near the rink, and they stepped out and started down the back toward the Plaza Hotel. Near the rink, they passed a Santa Claus, ringing his bell, standing near a chimney just as Jennifer had done at Rockefeller Center. Alex stopped, reached for his wallet and walked to the chimney. He nodded at the Santa, closed his eyes and dropped in some money. Santa HO-HO-HO'ED.

As Jennifer and Alex started for the rest rooms, Jennifer looked at him. "Do you believe in Santa Claus?" she asked.

"Absolutely. You?"

"I'm beginning to."

In the ladies room, Jennifer anxiously changed into her other clothes, folded her gold dress, placed it in the bag and inserted it into her locker.

When she appeared outside, Alex was waiting for her, beaming like a kid, anxious for an adventure.

Once the skates were rented and laced up, Alex led her toward the ice.

"I told you, I'm not that good," Jennifer said, worried.

Alex stepped out onto the ice and reached for her. "I

won't let you fall."

"Famous last words," she said, frowning.

She took his broad hand, and they waited for the rhythmic flow of the skaters before pushing away from the railing and joining them. He looked at her with amused surprise.

"You're doing great!" he said.

"I always feel like a clown when I'm on ice skates."

Skaters whizzed by, turned and whirled. Kids stammered across the ice, slipping and falling, reaching and giggling, while couples held hands and swayed. Jennifer struggled for a time, but as she felt Alex's sure hand and easy movement, she gradually stopped fighting the ice and found a comfortable pace.

Alex was noticeably delighted. "It makes me a little homesick for Harvey's Pond."

"So maybe you should go home."

He looked at her appealingly. "So, maybe I should."

"What did you and your father argue about?" Jennifer asked, feeling her left leg wobble unsteadily.

Alex took her arm and stabilized her. "Politics. Child rearing, sports, food, home improvement and movies. He's kind of a know-it-all."

"And you?"

He looked at her diffidently and shrugged. "Kind of a know-it-all."

"So, here's what you do. You sit down with him and you work out a system. Sometimes you let him be right. Sometimes he lets you be right. Whenever you can't agree on who should be right, you bring in a third party, like your mother or a good friend. The trick is, not to let the conversation get so out of control that you both become angry and threatened."

Alex looked at her in amazement. "Is it really that

easy?"

"No, not always, but with practice, I've seen it work."

He considered it. "I like it! Where did you learn that?"

"I was an office manager for a year when I got out of college."

"You'd be a great mother."

Jennifer's attention was suddenly drawn to a mother and her child, skating nearby. Neither were very accomplished skaters and they were making a valiant effort to stay on their feet. As Alex and Jennifer skated by, Jennifer looked over her shoulder and recognized the woman as being the same woman she'd seen at Rockefeller Center, earlier that evening. She had read the woman's thoughts. Jennifer remembered them verbatim.

*"Dear God, thank you for the apartment...please, I just need $200.00 to get me through the month... I know you can help me. I hope this dollar helps someone."*

Jennifer looked at the Santa Claus, suddenly getting an idea. "I'll be back in a minute," she said.

She released Alex's hand and drifted over to the railing while he watched, puzzled. She made her way back to her locker, opened her wallet and took out $200.00 in 20.00 dollar bills, put them in her pocket, then placed a $10.00 bill into her other pocket.

Back outside, she stepped over to the Santa Claus and dropped the $10.00 into his chimney. He nodded and thanked her.

She inched forward toward his white curly beard and whispered. "Can I trust you?"

He looked at her sternly, and stopped ringing his bell. "I'm Santa Claus! Of course you can trust me!"

Jennifer pulled out the $200.00 and showed it to him.

She pointed to the woman and child who were clumsily shuffling across the ice. "Can you give that woman this money?"

He looked at her over the top of his wire-rimmed spectacles. "Why don't you give it to her yourself?"

"I'd rather it came from you."

He lifted a white bushy eyebrow. "All right."

Jennifer gave him the money and he palmed it. "I'll take care of it," he said, winking at her.

As Jennifer started back toward the rink, she noticed that Alex was at the railing, still watching her.

"Asking Santa for something special on Christmas?" he asked.

Their eyes met again, his warm, hers hopeful, yet uncertain.

Alex pointed a playful accusing finger at her. "No thinking."

She laughed, and it was so liberating! It was a deep laugh that shook her entire body.

"That's the first time I've really seen you laugh, Jennifer."

She reached for his hand. "That's the first time you've called me Jennifer. Let's skate."

They circled the rink, feeling the cold wind on their faces, viewing the glorious buildings of the West Side, ghost-like in the snowfall, and the snow-covered trees, blurring, as they swept around the rink. Jennifer became aware that Alex kept easing his body closer to hers, until their hips joined. She pressed closer. She had never felt a thrill to compare with it—had never tasted wine as intoxicating—had never been as captivated by a delicious moment as the one that was stretching out before her into a timeless ecstasy.

She tilted her head to take in Alex's handsome face

and long hair, ruffled by the wind. Thoughts, questions and emotions struggled to rise up, but she stopped them. Nothing was going to snuff out this golden moment. "No thoughts," she said quietly to herself.

"Did you say something?" Alex asked.

"No. Nothing."

Jennifer's attention was suddenly diverted to a bundled-up kid, 10 or 11 years old. He was leading the mother and child she'd seen earlier. He made a beckoning motion toward the Santa Claus. Jennifer skated away from Alex and awkwardly arranged herself to view Santa as he handed the money to the woman, patting her hand warmly. Jennifer skated near the center of the rink for a better view, witnessing the woman's perplexed expression and her wide staring eyes as she examined the money. In gentle spasms, the woman wept in gratitude. She shook Santa Claus's hand, energetically, took her little daughter's hand and skated away, her face open and joyous.

Smiling to herself, Jennifer joined Alex again, and for the next 20 minutes, they skated across the ice effortlessly, making playful, imitative gestures of figure skaters, pretending, like children, that the secret world of pretend, discovery and imagination was theirs exclusively, and nothing in the world could take it away from them.

Then suddenly, there was a subtle shift in the air, and a burst of wind that changed the emphasis of the moment, as if someone had fumbled a priceless porcelain object and it fell, shattering.

Alex's cellphone went off like an alarm. It startled them both; shook them from the spell. Jennifer lost her balance. Alex reached for her, but it was too late. Her fall was swift and hard. As she fell, her right skate grazed Alex's left skate, just enough to pitch him precariously to his left. He couldn't maintain his balance and he desperately back-stepped, grasping at thc wind. He lost the battle and splashed to the ice, bracing himself with his hands. On impact, his cell phone leaped from his jacket and went sliding across the ice, ringing loudly.

He looked at Jennifer, concerned. "Are you okay?"

She nodded, sitting up, massaging her leg. "Yes... I think so."

On his knees, Alex scampered over to his cell phone, as several skaters shot by. He snatched it up and answered. "Hello!.. Yes, Valencia. I'm at Wollman Ice Skating Rink. What am I doing here? Well…"

Alex looked at Jennifer. She was being helped up by a female skater.

"It's a long story. Yes, I know. But … Look… Listen to me, Valencia." His voice grew firm. "I'm going back to the hospital. As soon as I'm sure Jason is okay, I'll meet you at your parents' apartment. Yes, I'll call before I come. Okay… goodbye."

Alex ended the call, pushed himself up and skated over to Jennifer.

"Valencia?" Jennifer said, forcing a pleasant expression.

He nodded.

"I have to get going, too," Jennifer said.

"Where?"

She slid her hands into her pocket and felt the business card that Dr. Phillips had given her. "I've got some plans."

Alex took her hand and they skated back toward the locker rooms.

After they had gathered their things and returned the skates, they started up the pathway toward the West Side. Alex saw a horse-drawn carriage approach. He waved, and it trotted toward them.

"What are you doing?" Jennifer asked.

"He's going our way."

The carriage drew up and Alex helped Jennifer inside. He climbed in and sat opposite her, offering her the red woolen blanket. She placed it over her legs and feet and instantly felt its warmth.

The cabby looked back. "Where to, folks, on this snowy night?" he said in an Irish accent.

"The Plaza Hotel," Jennifer said.

The carriage lurched forward. Alex sat with his arms folded, while Jennifer viewed Central Park, a winter wonderland.

"It's a beautiful night," she said.

"New York's a great town, isn't it? Sometimes I think anything is possible in this town. It's so big. So many different kinds of people, places and things to do. So many wonderful histories. I'd love to study more of its history."

"Maybe you will, after law school."

Alex lowered his head. "Valencia and her family have been good to me. Her father is the CEO of RayBrand Pharmaceuticals. I met her when I was working a construction job over on the east side. She said I looked like a cowboy."

"You could pass for one," Jennifer said, "if your hair was shorter."

"She's an attorney."

"She sounds like a nice woman," Jennifer said, "…and she has such a pretty name."

"Yeah, her mother's Spanish, her father was born in New York. Since I met her, I feel like I'm finally getting my life back together. I was just so lost and Jason needs a mother… needs a home. Valencia's parents love him like he was their own."

Jennifer smiled. "I'm happy for you, Alex. I really am."

Alex looked up, not meeting her eyes. "Are you going back to Willowbury?"

"Just to straighten out some loose ends. Then I'll probably leave."

"And go where?"

Jennifer was turning Dr. Phillips' card in her hand. "I'm going to start a new life. Have a completely different kind of adventure. I'm ready for that now. I'm ready to put my past behind me and move on."

"I hope you find what you're looking for, Jennifer," Alex said, still not looking at her.

The carriage slowly meandered through the park until it reached Central Park South and 59th Street. It paused, then the driver made the horse start trotting again, turning east, traveling toward Fifth Avenue. Jennifer caught sight of the Ritz Carlton, saw empty carriages waiting for tourists, saw strolling shoppers searching for yellow taxis. The horse's rhythmic steps reminded her of a grandfather's clock, winding down, announcing that time was running out. Strangely, she was almost relieved that they'd be parting soon. She was feeling a kind of emotional overload, as if she'd stuck her fingers inside a light socket.

But she also felt a little betrayed, although she knew she had no right to be. They had only just met and, anyway, it would all seem different in the morning on the flight back home. Her entire New York experience would probably float in and out of her consciousness like a dream, and then in the coming days and weeks, it would slowly be forgotten.

Alex looked directly at her, his eyes riveted on her face. There was an urgency in them, a kind of wild and lovely invitation. It was the kind of look that rattled her, that brought storms of pleasure and an urge to flee for her life.

"What do *you* want, Jennifer?" he asked, suddenly, aggressively.

She was stunned by his direct manner. "What do I want?"

"Yes. You asked me what I wanted. Why did you come to New York?"

They were approaching The Plaza Hotel and traffic began to snarl, horns blared.

Jennifer lifted her hand, as if searching for an answer. "Things happened. I just needed to get away."

"You must have been looking for something?"

Flustered, she averted his eyes, then quickly, irresistibly, returned to them. "I don't know!"

"How is it that we just found each other like this? Don't you wonder about that?"

She twisted uneasily. "I don't know anything about how or why things happen."

"But, this did happen. *We* happened."

"Yes, but…"

The carriage came to a stop.

Alex opened his hands. "Now what?"

"What do you mean? You have a fiancée. She's waiting for you."

"Are you going out with Dr. Phillips?"

She raised her shoulders and shook her head. "I might. He asked, and it *is* Christmas Eve."

The driver looked around. "We have arrived, folks."

Alex leaned forward, folding his hands. "That's right Jennifer. We've arrived. We have to make a decision."

# CHAPTER 15

Alex took her hand and led her out of the carriage. He paid the driver, then pulled her over toward the exterior of The Oak Room. He placed his hands on her shoulders, looking at her pointedly. "Jennifer, I'm the kind of guy who dribbles soup and sometimes coffee down the front of my shirt. I'll probably eat half your sandwich when you're not looking. I'm not a very good cook and I hate making the bed. But I'm loyal, I'm generous … and I love you."

Jennifer looked at him, struggling.

"Do you feel it, too, or is it just me? That…connection. That feeling of finally coming home after a long, long journey."

Jennifer tried to avoid his eyes, but she felt the gravitational pull of them, felt the incredible accident of their two worlds spinning in perfect orbit around each other, drawing closer to impact. She felt the desire to merge, to discover intimacy and love. "I don't know what you mean."

"Yes, you do, Jennifer. I see it in your eyes."

"Alex, you're scaring me."

"I'm scared, too, Jennifer. I don't know what the hell

happened to me when I saw you. But I've got to say it, Jennifer. I've got to. For the first time in years, I feel like I'm coming back to life. I mean, really back to life. Like I have a second chance, like I've been raised from the dead. Is it all just a coincidence? I don't know. Is it fate, some phase of the moon? I don't know and I don't care. All I know is I have never felt like this before. I have never known anything so quickly or so completely as I know that you and I are perfect together. I'm in love with you, Jennifer. I know it's fast and I know it's kinda scary, but there it is!"

Her heart raced. She pulled away and jerked up the collar of her coat, blinking fast. "Look… your son and your fiancée are waiting for you. You should go to them."

Alex searched her face. "Yes, I should. I know I should. But I'm standing here, looking at you, feeling like if I walk away, I'll be making the biggest mistake of my life. And if you go out with Dr. Phillips, you'll be making one of the biggest mistakes of your life."

"That's none of your business!"

"I've already made too many mistakes. I see that now. Jennifer… let's get Jason and go back to Willowbury together. Nothing would make him or me happier."

Jennifer stepped back, in frozen astonishment. "Alex, you're getting married in June! We've just met. You can't just be in love with me."

"'Whoever loved that loved not at first sight.'"

"What?"

"Christopher Marlowe."

"I don't know him."

"I'll teach you. You'll teach me a million things. We'll teach each other and Jason all kinds of things—wonderful things! We'll grow and learn together. Make love."

Jennifer turned away. Fear struck, like a cold stinging wind. His words set off so many conflicting and frightening emotions that she couldn't think.

She had trusted Lance and look what happened. She'd given him everything—believed in him, mourned his death, swore she'd never love again. Then she was betrayed! It was like being sliced open with a knife!

"Don't you see, Jennifer. We've just been given a gift. I know it! I feel it! Can't you?"

Jennifer trembled. Was it really a gift or just another ride around the merry-go-round of life? A world where it's so easy to deceive oneself into believing or feeling a certain way when in fact the opposite is true. It happens all the time!

She accepted the fact that she could be a better person, and she would try to be she would try her hardest. She also accepted that she'd been wrong about her parents and wrong about Lance's career. Okay, she believed that she could improve. But she wasn't ready to take the extraordinary leap of believing that she and this man, whom she'd just met, were in love and could somehow live happily ever after. No, she didn't believe that! Despite Mrs. Wintergreen, the visions from the past and the many coincidences, she didn't believe it. It was preposterous!

"Jennifer… what are you afraid of? Think back to when we first met—the first time we looked into each other's eyes. Didn't you know it then? Didn't you know it when we were talking together, skating together? Didn't you know we were in love and that we always will be? There's nothing to be afraid of, Jennifer."

She gave him a final troubled look, then walked away from him, toward the Hotel entrance. She heard him coming up from behind her, but she kept walking, purposely.

Alex seemed like a nice person, she had to admit that, and just looking at him aroused thoughts of love. They were definitely attracted to each other, but what did she know about raising a child? How could she ever compare herself to any woman, especially to a woman like Donna, who sounded like she had the confidence and innate ability to offer love and support?

"Jennifer… don't be afraid."

She couldn't go through the heartache again. What if one day she found out that Alex had actually been in love with Valencia all along, and because of her money and connections, he and Jason would have been much better off with her. She would undoubtedly make a much better wife and mother than Jennifer ever could.

She walked faster, breath coming fast, and Alex followed. "Jennifer… don't go!"

It was true that when she looked at Alex, she felt her heart open—felt a raw passion that she'd never felt before—felt her whole body open like a flower. But open to what? To the possibility of more pain and disappointment? It was so much easier to be alone! And yet, she had to admit that after meeting Alex, after holding Jason so tightly and warmly in her arms and feeling the beat of his heart against her chest, it would be difficult to be alone again. After all that, it would be so awful to be alone.

Alex seized her arm and turned her to face him. "Jennifer. Just say you want me to go away. Just say it, and I will. But before you do, think about what your future will be like if you walk away from us… from a life together with Jason and me."

Jennifer looked at him, nearly frantic with indecision.

That's when the full force of the truth struck her, with a terrible insight, shaking the foundation of her very soul. She stood stock-still, suddenly destroyed by the effort of suppressing an old truth that had never before found the light of recognition.

"Don't be afraid of love, Jennifer. After all, you were in love once before. You've been in love."

Her lips quivered. It took all her strength to speak. When she did, her voice was strained, filled with regret; her eyes dark and lifeless. "No, Alex. No... I wasn't in love. I was never truly in love with Lance. I didn't know it then, but I know it now."

She stared into Alex's searching eyes. "I held onto him because I was afraid. Terrified to look at myself for what I was: hurt and lost. I held onto him, desperately, and he was miserable. I held onto him and squeezed the life out of him and killed him in so many ways. But I never really loved him. I didn't really know what love is."

Her eyes filled with tears. "Please...leave me alone, Alex. I just need to be alone."

She turned slowly and walked away, up the red-carpeted stairs of The Plaza Hotel and into the lobby. She felt a gush of tears as she moved through the swirl of bustling crowds toward the elevators. She held in her emotion as she ascended to her floor, exited the elevator and ran to her room.

Inside, she closed the door and stood for a moment in the pulsing silence. She strolled unsteadily over to the window that looked out over the city and stared, through melting tears. The night sky was brightened by the city lights, and she saw the hint of a quarter moon, swimming through dark purple clouds. How would she ever be able to forgive herself?

"I'm so sorry, Lance… so sorry…"

The tears came slowly at first, almost as repressed sounds of grief. Then her shoulders began to shake violently, as if in spasm, and she began to cry out in uncontrollable anguish. She fell to her knees and toppled forward, burying her face into the carpet. Waves of despair rose to the surface and burst out into agonizing sobs.

# CHAPTER 16

Jennifer's eyes opened slowly; they felt sticky and heavy. She saw a blur of color and form, like some bizarre modern painting of cubes, broad lines and indefinite shapes. She slipped into consciousness hesitantly, testing it, like one would dip a couple of toes into a pool of water to check the temperature.

She was lying on the bed, covered by half of a luxurious quilted comforter, her bare feet sticking out one end, her head nearly covered by the other. What day was it? How long had she been sleeping?

As she lifted up, wiping her eyes and blinking about her hotel room, her memory slowly returned. She leaned back against the headboard, taking quick inventory of her surroundings, thoughts and feelings.

Generous sunlight streamed in from the windows, throwing quivering planks and squares onto the floor and on the end of the bed. Birds sailed by, banked left, soared high, then shot away, as if released by happiness into the distant blue sky.

Her thoughts were quiet, as quiet as the room, where she heard the occasional taxi horn below and the distant drone of an airplane. Church bells drifted in from a remote place and brought a reverent peace.

Images from the previous day began passing through her mind, as it threw back fragments of conversations, pictures and reactions. She closed her eyes and took them in, witnessing, remembering, feeling.

The first thing she noticed, remarkably, was that she felt quiet inside. The war that had been active inside of her for so many years had ended. The guns of anger and remorse were silent. Contentment and joy, which she had imprisoned with a crust of bitterness, now rose up, released; and like butterflies, they scattered into the freedom of rolling fields and flowers. She saw herself rise up, run, leap and flutter above those fields—felt the sunlight stun the world with its beauty, felt the call of newborn life. From inside, she stretched and expanded into that world, into the sunlight, seeping into the mystery of life.

She opened her eyes, threw back the comforter and stood up. There was such a feeling of lightness to her body! And where was that throbbing fear? She was perplexed by the lack of it—fear of facing the day and the world—fear of failing and feeling foolish. Fear of not having enough or of having too much. Suddenly, amazingly, she didn't care! It was so clear to her now that she had been tedious and irritating, like an old rusty gear on a bicycle that moved through the world grudgingly, scraping and squeaking.

She took a few steps forward, feeling as though she were taking brand new steps—steps that had never been taken before. Baby steps! That was okay. That was fine! She liked it. She felt young, girlish and as spirited as a puppy.

The time on her watch said 8:15. The date read December 25$^{th}$. Christmas Day! What would she do? What could she do? Anything! Absolutely anything she wanted! She was free to write the story of her life, anyway she wanted to, and she would do it with love, with generosity and with a playful sense of adventure.

In the shower, she pulled on a shower cap to preserve her hairdo, and let the warm water wash over her for 10 minutes while she sang, in a rather weak and shattering voice, *We Wish You a Merry Christmas.* She dried herself to a raucous version of *Jingle Bells*, and by the time she swung into her red terry cloth robe, she'd managed a fractured verse of *Joy to the World.*

In the closet, she reached for her burgundy dress and green silk scarf. As she dressed, she realized that she was ravenous. Visions of pancakes, sausages, eggs and hot coffee danced through her mind. She sat before the mirror and quickly applied makeup, doing her best to match Dale's artistry. As she worked, she thought of Angela, then, getting an idea, she smiled.

She tied the green scarf with a flourish around her neck and finished off her ensemble by snipping the stem of a red rose and placing it behind her right ear. It was one of the twelve red roses that had been delivered to her room the previous evening. As she examined herself in the mirror, she acknowledged that she no longer needed the designer dress to make her feel poised and confident. As she stared, she realized that the dress, that wonderful dress, had provided a kind of training wheels, helping her gain balance and self-assurance, allowing her to feel and experience the potential of her true beauty. Her body felt so comfortable now, as though she'd just met a new friend.

But why? What had really happened? Joy fell all around her, like confetti. She had released the past and had fallen in love! She was head-over-heels in love, crazy and rash in love, from the very moment she saw him! Alex! And, Jason, how she longed to hold him again! She was in love with the entire world!

She pulled on her black boots, snatched her coat and darted out of the room, pulling three additional red roses from the glass vase. Out the door, she skipped down the hallway and into the elevator, whose doors were open and waiting for her.

In the lobby, the aroma, atmosphere and celebration of Christmas were everywhere, with white Christmas lights reflected in chandeliers, and the smell of pine provoking grins. Cheerful faces wished her a "Merry Christmas" and, for the first time that she could remember since childhood, she wished them back a "Merry Christmas" and sincerely meant it. Her body seemed to sizzle like a sparkler whenever she said it, so she said it often to everyone she passed on her way out the front rotating doors.

Outside, the world was ablaze with sunlight, glistening off freshly fallen snow. Everything was scintillating with color and promise. It was a day to be unwrapped, discovered and enjoyed. Dogs barked, children hopped and danced. Early morning crowds wandered the streets, strolled through Central Park, or sat perched in horse-drawn carriages, shading their eyes against the glare, looking at the snow-covered world in wonder.

Jennifer's eventual goal was the hospital. She had to see Jason, find out where Alex was, and call him. She would tell him everything—explain it all—and he would believe her! He would understand!

But first, she had to make two stops. She descended the stairs and started toward Fifth Avenue. The air was crisp and still; the sidewalk had already been cleared of snow and sprinkled with salt. She scratched along until she came to St. Patrick's Cathedral. She crossed Fifth Avenue and approached it quietly, reverently. There was a hush as she started up the stairs. Not even a car rolled by. The great doors were closed and no one stirred as she stepped forward. When she reached the top stair, she leaned over and gently placed one rose on the spot where she'd last seen Lance.

"Thank you, Lance," Jennifer whispered. "I *will* let you go now. It's time for us both to move on and discover what's before us. I'll never forget you, and I'll always be grateful for what you did for me. God bless."

She turned and didn't look back as she descended the stairs and crossed the street, walking toward the majestic Christmas tree at Rockefeller Center.

The early crowd was sparse and quiet as they roamed the area, taking in the tree, the angels, and the colorful silk flags snapping in the wind. There were already ice skaters circling below, some with hands laced behind their backs, their red caps, green caps, like little domed candies stuck on their heads.

Jennifer walked to the spot where she'd met the Santa Claus, and she placed the second rose where he had allowed her to stand, to listen and to heal. A little girl, maybe 5 years old, bundled up in green and white, wobbled over, with questions in her deep blue eyes.

"What are you doing?" the little girl asked.

Her parents looked on from a short distance, noses and cheeks red from the cold. They, too, seemed curious.

Jennifer crouched down to the little girl's level. "I'm leaving a little present for Santa Claus."

The little girl was perplexed. She lifted her chubby hand and scratched her forehead. "Was he here?"

"Yes. He was here."

"Did you tell him what you wanted for Christmas?"

"Well… he seemed to know what I wanted without my having to ask."

"You must have been nice, then, or you would have got nothin'."

Jennifer laughed. "Okay… You've got me there."

The little girl turned around and ran back to her parents. Jennifer waved and started off toward the hospital.

She was nearly out of breath when she arrived at the hospital front desk. She signed in and hurried to the elevator. As it ascended to the 7th floor, Jennifer lifted the rose and smelled its sweetness, studied the elegant petals, a flower more perfect and attractive than any she'd ever seen before. The richness of color and the delicate satin-like texture were spellbinding. Jennifer looked up to watch the floor lights jump from 3 to 4 to 5 to 6 and finally to 7. Perhaps Alex would be there, playing with Jason, maybe dressing him in preparation for the big day. Her heart pounded with anticipation.

She left the elevator, walking rapidly down the quiet hallway, smelling coffee and disinfectant. As she approached Jason's room, Nurse Flanders came toward her from the opposite direction. They immediately recognized each other and stopped outside Jason's room. Jennifer noticed that the door was closed.

"Merry Christmas!" Jennifer said, brightly. "You're working a lot of hours."

Nurse Flanders looked concerned and waited a moment before speaking. "Merry Christmas. Yes. We're short-staffed."

"So how is Jason this morning?"

Nurse Flanders folded her arms. "He passed all his

tests with flying colors. The doctors, of course, still don't understand it."

"May I see him?"

"He's been released."

"Released?"

"Yes, his father came and got him early this morning. He said they had a lot to do before Christmas dinner with his fiancée's family. He said they were all going to East Hampton for a few days. Her family has a house there."

The hand that was carrying the rose dropped suddenly to Jennifer's side. A single petal fell to the floor. "Oh…" Jennifer said, weakly.

"Did you know they were engaged?"

"Yes… I…" Jennifer's voice trailed off into silence. "How was Jason?"

"He asked about you."

Jennifer looked up, pleased. "Did he?"

"Yes, he told his father that he couldn't leave, because you were coming back to see him."

"What did his father say?"

"He didn't say anything. But Jason kept repeating it, while his father dressed him and gathered up his things. Finally, his father told him that you fully intended to see him and that maybe someday you would."

"And… Jason accepted that?" Jennifer asked.

Nurse Flanders shook her head slowly. "No, he didn't. He pouted and insisted that he wasn't going to leave until you showed up."

"How long ago did they leave?"

"About two hours ago."

Jennifer's shoulders dropped.

"Jennifer… it is Jennifer, isn't it?"

Jennifer nodded.

"Working in a hospital, I see so many things. So many things I wish I could change. So many things happen and I don't understand why they happen or why things are the way they are, but I have learned one thing: miracles do happen, and sometimes they catch me off-guard. A visit from a friend, a phone call, a poem written, a song sung, a firm commitment to finding a cure for a difficult illness. They're all miracles because someone cared—someone reached out. You and Jason—you and Alex—love at first sight. Don't you think?"

Jennifer smiled. "Jason thinks I saved his life, but, in fact, he saved mine."

A bell rang from a patient's room. "I've got to go, Jennifer," Nurse Flanders said. "Have a wonderful holiday."

Nurse Flanders started off down the hallway, then stopped and turned. "Oh, by the way, on the way out, I heard Jason tell his father that he would find you again."

Jennifer managed a brief smile. "Thank you."

Nurse Flanders entered another room.

Jennifer looked at the closed door to Jason's old room, thought for a moment, then opened it and went inside. She closed it gently, adjusted her eyes to the bright sunlight and took in the quiet surroundings: the empty walls where Jason's drawings had hung, the bare windowsill, devoid of cards, the empty bed.

She could see Jason's large eyes, hopeful, pleading with her to return. She could still feel his warm, springy little body against hers; feel that sense of peace that comes with being wanted, and belonging to someone.

She saw Alex, with all that hair, and the passion and enthusiasm of a mad poet, gripping her shoulders, staring at her with those burning eyes. It would have been a daring life, a leap off a tall cliff, but one she would have relished. She hadn't been ready last night. Now she was. She was ready to take that leap, but it was too late.

How do you forget those who enter your life with the quiet force of spring and change your inner landscape so completely, change the cold, seemingly unconquerable voices of winter into sighs of hope, recognition and longing?

She stepped toward the bed, paused for a moment, remembering thankfully all that they had done for her, then slowly, she laid the third rose on the bed. A moment later, she turned and left the room.

Jennifer walked easily back to The Plaza Hotel, delighting in the decorated windows, the bright blue sky and the fresh air. She found a diner that was open and went in, joining others at the crowded counter, people dressed in flannel shirts, or cozy sweaters, corduroy pants and colorful hats. The red vinyl booths were stuffed with families and friends, all grins and zeal, plunging into pancakes, waffles and bagels, sharing stories of shopping, theater and restaurants. They all looked so happy—so content to be with each other.

Hunger gnawed at her stomach. She couldn't remember ever being so hungry. She ordered pancakes, eggs and bacon, with coffee—two cups of coffee. She ate slowly, savoring each bite, while the silver Christmas tree in the corner blinked and dazzled, and the music coming from overworked ceiling speakers scratched out a variety of Christmas carols. It was the perfect place to be, sharing the simplicity of the diner and her splendid breakfast with other tourists, New Yorkers and the two waiters, who wore Santa Claus hats and handed out candy canes to the children. Jennifer didn't feel isolated or lonely; on the contrary, she felt comfortable and connected to them all, as if they were good friends, sitting in her own dining room.

An elderly man, seated on the stool to her left, turned. He had a weathered, kindly face that reminded her of her father.

"Are you going home for Christmas?" he asked.

She smiled, warmly. "Yes. Yes, I am going home."

# CHAPTER 17

Jennifer drove a rented emerald-green Ford Escort along Collier's Road toward Willowbury. She glanced at the snow-heavy pines and quiet snowy hills. A frosty white afternoon sun was playing hide and seek with lazy clouds, making the horizon crimson and gold, the colors of her gorgeous room at The Plaza Hotel. Curls of gray smoke rose from little homes far away, where windows glowed back at her like tiny fires. She passed through the covered bridge and, on the other side, saw the distant white church steeple that gave her a rush of excitement, because Harvey's Pond was just ahead and she would soon be home.

It seemed like weeks since she'd left, and it had only been two days! Everything was more picturesque, more beautiful than she remembered, as if the entire landscape had just been given a fresh coat of paint. Birds lifted toward the sky in unpredictable flight, defining the air with their darting bodies, skimming over the heads of dogs that romped and barked at them, over the colorful hats of children who tore across the land leaping and falling. Snowmen appeared, a kite trembled high over bare black trees, and the moan of a train whistle echoed.

It felt so good to be home.

As she neared Harvey's Pond, she became acutely aware that there was a lilting gentleness about the landscape that soothed and uplifted her. It met the sky seamlessly, in astonishing silence.

On the plane she'd had much time to reflect and think about the future. She was eager to take on the responsibilities and challenges of re-building her shop. It would be a wonderful adventure and she'd improve it in every way. Perhaps she'd add a bookstore and café, as Alex's wife had done. It excited her to think of people gathering to read and talk; sip coffee; sit with their children, spouses or dates. She loved the idea of allowing people to use the shop to sell muffins, candy, cookies or pastries to help raise money for community events or school projects. She even considered adding an apartment above or next to the shop. She could rent it out to an employee, or even use it herself.

She grinned broadly when she saw Harvey's Pond, a brilliant sun lying across it. She watched skaters pass through patterns and shadows, their arms raised, their shiny faces lifted toward the sky. Jennifer remembered her conversations with Mrs. Wintergreen and the many gifts she'd received. Would she ever see her again? It no longer mattered to her if the woman existed or not. Much of what had happened to her still seemed like a dream, but she couldn't deny the change she felt inside—it was real! She couldn't ignore that she had fallen in love with life, and with Alex and Jason. It was *their* love of *her* that had finally cracked her open—that had awakened her from a deep sleep, by the thunder of love. She would always be grateful to them for that.

On the plane, she'd decided not to tell the Hartmans that she'd seen their son in New York. She felt it was something that Alex would do in his own time, when he felt ready.

As she approached town, she turned left on Appleton Way and drove a mile or so down the two-lane road leading to a three-story apartment complex. She entered the parking lot, found a free space, and parked the car. She got out, opened the passenger door and took out four brightly wrapped presents. With a little kick to the door, it closed securely, and she started toward the entrance. Inside, she walked along the hallway of blue cinder block walls, until she found the elevator. She took it up to the second floor and exited left, searching until she found apartment 2D. Shifting the presents to her left arm, she clumsily found the doorbell and pressed it lightly.

A moment later, the door opened and Jennifer looked into Angela's surprised face.

"Ms. Taylor?"

"Merry Christmas, Angela."

They stood for a moment in an awkward silence while Angela looked first at Jennifer's pleasant and friendly face, then at her hairdo, and then at the beautifully wrapped gifts.

Finally, Jennifer spoke. "Pardon me for barging in on you like this at Christmas, but I just wanted to drop these presents off and tell you that I'm going to keep you on salary while the shop is under construction."

Angela was speechless.

Jennifer offered the presents. "These are for you and your family. Just small things, really, but I wanted to get you and your family something."

Angela remained still.

Jennifer leaned forward and Angela finally took the

gifts. "I don't know what to say," Angela said, touched.

"I got them at a shop at The Plaza Hotel," Jennifer said. "It was so much fun, only I didn't know how many people, I mean family members, are actually living with you. I remember you talking about your daughter and your father. Well, anyway, I brought four gifts, just in case there's someone else. I mean, you can always use another gift, right?" Jennifer said, nervously, trying for a joke.

"The Plaza Hotel?" Angela said, her eyes moistening.

"I was away, in New York."

"New York?"

"Something came up, kind of suddenly."

"Thank you, Ms. Taylor…I just don't know what to say."

"You don't have to say anything, Angela."

"You look so…different. Beautiful… Younger. I mean, you looked young before, you know, but… well,"

"I understand."

"I tried to call you when I heard about the accident," Angela said. "Are you all right?"

"Oh, yes. I'm doing great."

A little girl with dark hair, a pudgy face and gorgeous brown eyes appeared. Her dress was pink, her shoes red. She snuggled up to Angela's legs and stared up at Jennifer, suspiciously.

"Hi," Jennifer said, cheerfully.

"Are you that mean woman who works with Mommy?" the little girl asked.

Angela's face flushed with embarrassment. "Oh God! Mariah!"

Jennifer laughed. "I'm not so mean…"

"I'm so sorry," Angela said.

"It's okay, really. May I meet your father?"

"Oh, yeah, sure," Angela said, backing away. "It's just that, well, I just thought that you didn't want to meet my father or daughter, so I never invited you."

"Forgive me, Angela. Forgive me for all those silly things I said. I would love to meet your family."

For the next half-hour, Jennifer, Angela, Mariah and Angela's father, Juan Garcia, ate cookies and drank hot chocolate. They talked about Jennifer's trip to New York, Juan's grandchildren in Florida, and what Jennifer and Angela were going to do with the new shop.

At 5:00 o'clock, darkness had settled in and Jennifer said she had one more stop to make. Angela walked her to the door. Before Jennifer left, Angela took her hand and, with grateful eyes, kissed her on both cheeks.

"Thank you, Ms. Taylor. Thank you for the presents and for coming by. I never would have believed it. You've made me so happy."

Jennifer nibbled on her lower lip. "Have I? Have I really?"

"Yes…"

Jennifer took her hand. "We'll make the shop better than ever, Angela, and after a few months, if we don't spend too much on frivolous things like laptops, hot chocolate and makeup, we'll give ourselves a raise."

They embraced and Jennifer left.

Jennifer drove slowly along Shepherd Lane, the street where the Hartmans lived, aware that her throat was dry and her palms were moist on the steering wheel. The moon was perched on the horizon, as if watching her, curious to know what the outcome of the visit would be.

She saw the tall firs and pines, the Christmas lights, the plastic Santa, reindeer and manger scene on the spread of snow, and noticed three cars parked in the circular driveway. Creeping forward, she gathered courage, then turned and stopped. She switched off the engine and sat in the stillness for a moment, slowly feeling the cold seep in. Finally, she pushed the door open and stepped out into the frigid night air, quietly closing the door behind her. Strolling down the walkway toward the front door, she heard music coming from the house. She couldn't make out what it was, but it sounded festive. At the front door, she lifted her shoulders and gently relaxed them, then pressed the glowing yellow doorbell and waited. It seemed an eternity until the door opened and she looked into Gladys Hartman's astonished face.

"Jennifer! I don't believe it! What happened to you?!"

"Well… I…"

Gladys turned sharply and called. "J. D., get over here, now!"

Gladys came forward and gave Jennifer a big hug. "I'm so glad you're okay. We were so worried."

Gladys led her into the house and closed the door, just as J. D. Hartman came heavily across the living room, his face an expression of delighted shock.

"Jennifer Taylor!"

Jennifer folded her hands, but J. D. wrapped his meaty arms around her and gave her a bear hug, nearly squeezing the air out of her body.

"I don't believe it! We were worried sick!" he said, holding her at arm's length and looking at her. "Well… you look fantastic! Doesn't she, Gladys!"

Gladys scrutinized her. "You look fabulous! I just love your hair!"

Jennifer worked to recover her composure. "I decided to accept your offer to have dinner… that is, if you haven't had it already, and if the offer is still open."

"Heck no! I mean, no, we haven't eaten, and, yes the offer is still open," J. D. said, boisterously. "It's cooking now! Well, this is just perfect, isn't it, Gladys!? I mean, how could this Christmas be any more perfect!"

Gladys folded her hands and clasped them to her chest. "It's the best Christmas that I can remember, J. D." Gladys faced Jennifer, struggling not to show emotion. "Jennifer… in addition to your being here, joining us for Christmas dinner, our son, Alex, and our grandson, Jason, are also here! They have come home."

Jennifer froze. "I beg your pardon?"

J. D. stepped forward. "Yes, Jennifer. Alex and Jason showed up a little over an hour ago. They've been living in New York for the past seven months. We couldn't believe it," J. D. said, wrapping his arm around Gladys' shoulder and pulling her close. "We just couldn't believe it!"

Jennifer backed away. "Oh, well, I should be going then."

"Going!?" J. D. asked. "What do you mean, going?"

"You'll want to be with your son and grandson," Jennifer said, craning her neck, looking for them. "You'll want to get to know his fiancée."

"Fiancée?!" Gladys and J. D. exclaimed, perplexed. "What fiancée?"

"… Alex is supposed to be married in June."

J. D. and Gladys exchanged puzzled glances. "Really?"

Gladys said, "Jennifer, Alex didn't tell us anything about a fiancée. He did tell us that he met a girl—a wonderful girl—he even said he was in love, but he didn't say anything about getting married."

"That's because I was waiting for the right moment,"

Alex said, standing in the doorway between the kitchen and the living room. He wore a bright red sweater, jeans and brown cowboy boots. "Hi, Jennifer. I told Valencia the truth. I told her I fell in love with you. What else could I do?"

Jennifer turned slowly to meet him, struggling for balance. Their eyes met and Jennifer allowed her eyes to linger on his face, his hair, his eyes. She felt a desperate relief.

"I'm not in love with Valencia, Jennifer."

Suddenly, Jason burst out from between Alex's legs and charged Jennifer, yelling joyfully. J. D. and Gladys looked on incredulous, as Jennifer crouched and Jason rushed into her arms, nearly knocking her to the floor. She gave him a huge kiss and hug.

"I said I'd find you again," Jason said.

"So you did, Jason. So you did!"

"Will someone please tell me what the hell is going on?!" J. D. asked, shooting glances first to Alex and then to Jennifer.

While Jennifer held Jason, Alex started toward her. "It's all very simple, Dad, Jennifer and I met in New York and now we have a lot of things to talk about."

Jennifer rose to her feet, smiling, clasping Jason's little hand.

"Talk?" Gladys asked, her eyes glistening with happiness.

"Yes, Mom," Alex said, gently touching Jennifer's face. "Things happened pretty fast down there."

Jennifer smiled. "Yes, wonderful things."

J. D. stood amazed. "This is incredible! This is fantastic! This is… is…

Gladys interrupted. "…is wonderful!"

J. D. lifted his hands. "Then, what's to be done?"

Jennifer lifted her face to Alex. He leaned and kissed her. Jason snuggled in between them, grinning up at his grandparents.

Gladys took J. D.'s hand and led him out of the living room. Just before they entered the kitchen, they turned to catch a final look. Jennifer and Alex were still kissing. Jason ran toward his grandparents. In one sweeping motion, J. D. joyfully gathered him up into his arms.

Gladys looked at J. D. and whispered. "They won't be talking long, J. D."

He whispered back. "They aren't doing much talking right now, Gladys."

They looked at each other, then to Jason, and then they nodded once, in final agreement, before retreating into the kitchen.

# EPILOGUE

It's December 10th, and I'm sitting in the back office of Cards & Stuff Café writing this, while Angela and Alex are taking care of the customers. A few minutes ago, I heard Mrs. Stanton's exuberant voice, asking for a second cappuccino, and I'm sure Alex told her that she should cut back, because he's been telling her that ever since the shop reopened in early April. He's the only person who can get away with telling her that, because she loves him, and has loved him ever since he was a child. When she learned that Alex and I were in love and were going to be married, she dropped all the charges against me (telling me privately that she hadn't really hurt herself) and even offered us a loan to help rebuild the shop. We declined, of course, but we did take her up on the offer to pay the high school kid, Rick Haymore, extra money to come by and shovel the walk at 6 o'clock in the morning on snowy days, so it's clear for her to walk at 6:30. That put her in charge of the whole operation and took us off the hook.

Alex and I were married on February 1st. The month of January was like a whirlwind. On January 2nd, Alex and I started securing loans, an architect and contractors for the rebuilding efforts. We were delighted and very moved when so many people in town came forward, offering time, labor and materials, and within a little over three months, the shop was ready for the grand opening.

Around the same time, I also learned that I was pregnant. The baby is due on Dec. 24th, an auspicious day for sure.

Around the middle of February, just after our one-week honeymoon in New York, Alex began teaching history again at the high school. Sometimes he gets so excited and enthusiastic about his teaching that he keeps us both up until midnight, discussing his ideas, the students and all the things he wants to accomplish. His enthusiasm is contagious. We grow closer every day and are constantly discovering new and wonderful, and sometimes frightening things about each other. He does, in fact, dribble soup down the front of his sweaters and he often finishes my sandwiches when I'm not looking. But then, he has to put up with my cold feet, even in summer, my inclination to take pills at the slightest hint of any illness or sniffle, and my persistent tardiness, which I've tried to correct at least 100 times.

Alex and his father are making improvements in their relationship, although they still vehemently disagree on politics, sports, child rearing, food and religion. Okay, so it's a work in progress.

Jason is a handful, and a treasure. I'm also discovering new things about him every day. One thing is a constant: he's an adventurer and a wanderer. He roams the woods and fields and knows every stream, animal hole and cave within a mile. He talks to deer and raccoons and runs with the birds in spring and autumn, arms outstretched and flapping. Alex and I are convinced that he'll grow up to be a forest ranger, a smoke jumper or an environmentalist, because he loves the earth with a passion that constantly amazes and inspires me.

The Hartmans love the shop. Gladys often volunteers in the gift shop, bookstore and café, and has been known to drink two or three espressos in an afternoon. She gets so wired that sometimes she dances to the Latin CDs that Angela purchased and plays in the late afternoons when the shop fills with teachers and students. J. D. says she makes a spectacle of herself, but I've seen him come by, sneak a peek at her rotating hips, and grin pleasurably if he thinks no one is looking.

Dale, the hairdresser, moved to town in August, just as Mrs. Wintergreen had predicted. He loves it, and his shop is thriving. His prices are high, and I've argued with him about that many times, but he still gives me a better haircut than anyone else I've ever gone to, so I give in, albeit under protest. He and Angela began dating in October and, although it seems like an odd match to me, they seem happy together. Angela says he's very fond of Mariah, and he is teaching Angela new makeup tricks. She thinks he's "the one." I hope so.

As I'm writing this, snow is beginning to cover the pines and blanket the ground. I remember, so distinctly, nearly a year ago when I walked to Harvey's Pond and met Mrs. Wintergreen. I have not seen her since, although Jason said he spoke to her just after Thanksgiving, when she passed through town on her way to Boston. He said she asked about me, and she told Jason to tell me that an open heart is the greatest of gifts. Jason thought it had something to do with open heart surgery, and although I've explained it to him, he likes the surgery idea much better.

*Christmas Ever After* is selling well in the shop and online. I have an eReader and Alex hates it, often declaring that I'm "a traitor to real books and book publishers everywhere." Alex and I wrote the book together, mostly on weekends, and whenever we had a few spare moments. I don't pretend to understand how it all happened, but it did happen, and I wanted to write it down and share it with others.

I hope you enjoyed the story. Perhaps it will resonate with you and give you some of the discovery and happiness that I experienced. Whatever you believe, and wherever you find yourself this Christmas, I sincerely hope it is the merriest of Christmases, filled with great blessings, joy and love.

Jennifer Taylor Hartman

The End

CPSIA information can be obtained
at www.ICGtesting.com
Printed in the USA
LVHW041515060919
630195LV00026B/713/P

9 781490 545196